TAILS OF THE BRONX

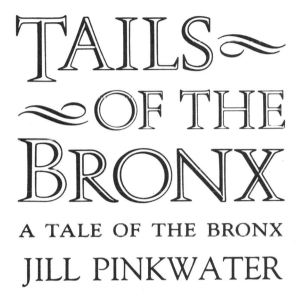

TAILS OF THE BRONX

A TALE OF THE BRONX

JILL PINKWATER

MACMILLAN PUBLISHING COMPANY
COLLIER MACMILLAN CANADA   TORONTO
MAXWELL MACMILLAN INTERNATIONAL PUBLISHING GROUP
NEW YORK   OXFORD   SINGAPORE   SYDNEY

Macmillan Publishing Company
866 Third Avenue
New York, NY 10022
Collier Macmillan Canada, Inc.
1200 Eglinton Avenue East Suite 200
Don Mills, Ontario M3C 3N1
FIRST EDITION
Printed in the United States of America
10 9 8 7 6 5 4 3 2 1
The text of this book is set in 11 pt. Goudy Old Style.
Book design by Christy Hale
Library of Congress Cataloging-in-Publication Data
Pinkwater, Jill.
Tails of the Bronx : a tale of the Bronx / by Jill Pinkwater. —
1st ed.
p.   cm.
Summary: In their search for a group of missing cats,
a group of children in the Bronx encounters
the problems of homelessness firsthand.
ISBN 0-02-774652-6
[1. Bronx (New York, N.Y.)—Fiction.   2. Neighborhood—Fiction.
3. Homeless persons—Fiction.]   I. Title.
PZ7.P6336Tai   1991
[Fic]—dc20   90-48914

To my sister, Phyllis Halpern

CONTENTS

ONE

FRIENDS

There is no place on earth like the Bronx. It's part of New York City, and I live there. My name is Loretta Bernstein. I live on Burnridge Avenue between the two 112s—112th Street and 112th Avenue.

I am ten years old. I am a short, skinny, Jewish, African-American kid. My ancestors came from Ethiopia and were all black and Jewish, too. We are called Falashas and are descended from the Queen of Sheba.

It's easy to tell who I am in a crowd because I wear big, round, red-framed eyeglasses all of the time and my official forest ranger hat most of the time.

My claim to fame, besides having a famous ancestor, is that I am the only kid in the neighborhood who is going to be a forest ranger. I started working on my career when I was still practically a baby, studying the flora and fauna—that's plants and animals—at the New York Botanical Garden in the Bronx. I could identify most of the plants in the Perennial Garden long before I knew the names of most of my relatives. My friends say I will never become a ranger because it would mean that I would have to leave the Bronx. It *is* a problem, but I'll cross that bridge when I come to it. Meanwhile, a forest ranger is what I'm going to be.

Last year I earned two Master of Bugology certificates at the annual New York Botanical Garden Bug Hunt. I collected the most bugs *and* the greatest variety of bugs. It was no accident I won the contest. I've been on every one of the 250 acres of the Botanical Garden. I know where the bugs live, what they eat—and what eats them.

Everything important that has happened to me in my life has taken place in the Bronx—most of it on my block. That's because of the first Big Rule on Burnridge. If you're under eleven, you are not allowed off the block alone, except to go to school. *Alone* means without an adult. Being with a bunch of other kids doesn't count—no matter how many are with you.

The second Big Rule is: Be home before the streetlights go on. This is a tricky rule, because streetlights do not get turned on by a switch or even a timer. They're worked by photoelectric cells. That means darkness and light turn them on and off. On cloudy days, especially in winter, the lights will sometimes kick on as early as four o'clock—catching everyone in the middle of important games or conversations. When that happens, there is a whole lot of yelling and screaming as kids race home. I've told my parents that it isn't fair for us kids to have our lives run by the weather. They tell me that nobody ever said life would be fair.

More than a hundred kids live on the block. I know them all, but mostly I hang out with my particular friends. Susan Quinn is my best friend. Her claim to fame is that she is the biggest nine-and-a-half-year-old in the entire neighborhood—and that includes both 112th Street *and* 112th Avenue, our school, and the Grand Concourse, which is nearby. She may be the biggest nine-and-a-half-year-old in the Bronx, but we haven't checked out the whole Bronx yet. The Bronx is a very large place. On the other hand, Susan Quinn is a very large kid—fat and tall. She'd get me if she heard me say *fat*. She prefers to describe herself as much bigger than usual.

Susan Quinn likes to be called Suzie Q. Suzie Q is a very tough kid. Nobody crosses her. When she was in third grade, a sixth-grade boy began calling Suzie Q "Gorilla" whenever he saw her. One day, when she had had enough, Suzie Q wrestled the kid to the ground and sat on his back for an entire lunch period. She made him say "Suzie Q" one thousand times. She made me do the counting. That was the last time anyone teased Suzie Q—to her face, at any rate.

The Raven is also a good friend of mine, even though he usually hangs around with older kids. He's Suzie Q's older brother. He's twelve, which means he's allowed off the block by himself. His claim to fame is that he is the only graffiti artist in the Bronx who works from a wheelchair. The Raven says his sitting position gives him an advantage because it puts him a couple of feet below where most of the other kids have used up blank wall space. The Raven does not draw on buses or subway cars or houses where people live. He says he is an urban artist who specializes in making the Bronx more beautiful, so mostly he decorates the walls of abandoned buildings. There are lots of those in our part of the Bronx.

The Raven is his graffiti name. It's also what he likes to be called. Sean is his real name, but he hasn't answered to it since he got his first spray can. The Raven is a major fan of Edgar Allan Poe, the famous Bronx poet. The Raven took his name from one of Poe's popular poems. Now that The Raven is allowed to travel around the Bronx alone, he visits Poe Park and Poe Cottage at least once a month.

The Raven's never been able to walk, but he gets around faster than any kid I've ever seen. He has racing wheels on his chair and always wears fingerless leather gloves so he can do wheelies or take off at top speed whenever he wants to. The Raven can go from a dead standstill to thirty miles an hour in less than ten seconds. He's faster than some cars in the neighborhood. The Raven's arms are very strong. He is the only kid on the block who can catch and hold on to Calvin when Calvin starts to run.

Calvin isn't exactly a friend. He's my brother. He's seven. It's my job to mind Calvin when we're outside. This isn't easy because Calvin's claim to fame is how fast he can run. He is the fastest runner at P.S. 46, our school. He can beat even the oldest kid on our block. When Calvin wants to leave the block, he leaves. Usually he just runs down 112th Street, along the Grand Concourse, up 112th Avenue, and back down Burnridge to our apartment house. On our block, that's a major crime for kids. So far Calvin has not had the nerve to cross any streets. Once he starts doing that, I think my parents are going to make me tie a rope around his waist and lead him around like a dog.

Anyway, if The Raven is around, Calvin can hardly make it to the corner even if he has a head start of half a block. This is important to me because if the Neighborhood Watch sees Calvin leave the block, a report is made to my parents. If Calvin leaves the block, I get the same punishment Calvin gets because I'm supposed to be minding him. To mind someone in the Bronx means to keep him in sight and out of trouble. No excuses. It's not fair, because Calvin is so fast and sneaky, but life in the Bronx can be tough.

That's what Julio Rodriguez says all the time. Julio's claim to fame is that he is the best-dressed, cleanest person on the block, in the neighborhood, in the Bronx, probably in New York City—all five boroughs—maybe in the United States. The Raven says it isn't normal for a kid Julio's age to be so unwrinkled and clean. Julio is ten, like me. If five of us go on an adventure in the alleys and basements of Burnridge Avenue, four of us will end up covered with dirt and grime and soot. Sometimes one of us will rip a shirt or a jacket on something sharp. Not Julio. Never Julio.

Julio wears a silver chain around his neck. On it is his good luck charm—a small, silver rabbit's foot. His grandmother gave it to him. He says it protects him from bad guys and dirt. We make fun of Julio and his magic charm. Julio doesn't care. He says as long as he stays clean and pressed and free of bruises, we can laugh all we want. Julio insists that since he started wearing the charm, not one bad kid in the Bronx has bothered him.

I like Julio. He and I plan adventures together. He calls us co-conspirators and says we share a psychic wavelength. That means we think alike. Julio is the smartest kid I know. He studies the dictionary and learns three new words every night. Sometimes, when Julio uses two or three of his dictionary words in a sentence, the rest of us have no idea what he is talking about. Julio also speaks Spanish—mostly to his grandmother. He says that considering the neighborhood we live in, there is

13

no excuse for all of us not to know at least one language besides English. He even thinks Suzie Q should learn Gaelic.

The first time he told her that, Julio had to explain to Suzie Q that Gaelic is the ancient language of Ireland, the place Suzie Q's ancestors came from. Suzie Q was sitting on Julio's stomach as he spoke because she thought he had said "eat garlic" not "speak Gaelic." Suzie Q took it as an insult and threw Julio to the ground as punishment.

"Your rabbit's foot didn't protect you from Suzie Q," I said after Julio had brushed himself off.

"Suzie Q is not a bad guy," he said. "She is simply a monolingual lout of my acquaintance." Then a clean, unwrinkled Julio smiled at Suzie Q and sauntered off. An embarrassed Suzie Q ignored his remark.

That night I looked up *monolingual* and *lout* in the dictionary. I kept my findings to myself. I like Julio.

Anthony DeRosa is my next-door neighbor and the best-looking boy in the Bronx. He is an only child. We are the same age and have always lived in the same building. Anthony and I are like brother and sister. We're also very good friends. This means we argue a whole lot but never stay mad for long.

Anthony's claim to fame is that he knows more about the people on the block than they know about themselves. He spends huge amounts of his time collecting the life stories of everyone he meets. Anthony is the favorite kid of all the older people on Burnridge. He's really interested in listening to them—especially if they are talking about their troubles. They tell him *everything*—about themselves and about others. In their eyes, Anthony DeRosa can do no wrong—and believe me, he does plenty.

Kids tell Anthony things, too—secret stuff they never thought they'd say out loud. When Anthony listens to someone, he really *listens*. I don't know how he does it, but as soon as he fixes those big brown eyes on someone, that person begins talking. He's our main source of block information—like a daily news broadcast. I figure that someday Anthony will be a famous psychiatrist or detective or FBI agent or spy or reporter. He certainly has the right talent.

Finally, there is Rochelle Firestone. I can't exactly call her a friend, she's just with us most of the time—uninvited. Rochelle's claim to fame is that she is the richest kid and the worst snob on the block. She says her family is homesteading on Burnridge, like pioneers. I remember the first time Rochelle announced that her family was "turning the tide" and opening our block to what she called other upwardly mobile families. We turned our backs on her and walked away.

"Does she think the rest of us are downwardly mobile?" Julio asked, looking angry.

"What does that mean?" asked Calvin.

"That we're losers," Julio answered.

"My dad says that even though the families on Burnridge are hardworking, most of us are just a few paychecks away from being homeless," said Suzie Q.

"He said 'used to be,' " The Raven corrected his large baby sister. "Now that we have the Neighborhood Association, we're not so . . . so . . . . "

"Vulnerable," Julio helped.

"Still, it's scary," I said. "What if my dad lost his job?"

"Mommy works, too," said Calvin.

"My mom isn't working now because of the baby." Suzie Q sounded very worried.

Rochelle showed up, so we changed the topic. None of us wanted to give her the satisfaction of knowing we were upset by anything she did or said. But we've talked about our worries

15

many times since. It helps to have friends you can share things with—even awful things.

Anyway, back to Rochelle. None of my friends really likes her much, but since her first day on the block, she's hung on to Suzie Q like a leech. Rochelle bribes Suzie Q with junk food. In exchange, Suzie Q doesn't let the rest of us destroy Rochelle when she says something snotty or nasty. Remarks come out of Rochelle's mouth at the rate of about four or five an hour. Some days Suzie Q has to really work to earn her candy bars and pizza slices. If it weren't for Suzie Q, Rochelle would have been history a week after her family moved here.

My friends and I do a lot of hanging around the block together. Not a single one of us has a personal television, or computer, or stereo system. As you have probably figured out, there isn't a whole lot of extra money on Burnridge Avenue. Two of us have bicycles, and we all have our own radios—small ones, not Bronx Blaster Boxes. Except Rochelle, of course. She has a room full of every toy that has ever been advertised on television. I saw her room once when she first moved in. It was like visiting a store. We played for about an hour with Rochelle's stuff—until I got bored and restless. It was a new experience for me. I had never been bored in my life. I began questioning Rochelle.

I discovered what Rochelle didn't have was anything practical—like the things needed for playing in the street. She didn't have a pink Spalding ball, or a clothesline rope, or white chalk, or a wax-filled bottle cap, or jacks, or marbles, or skates with metal wheels. Rochelle didn't even own a yo-yo. It was pitiful. Unfortunately, her mother did have an empty can, and that's why I got banned from Rochelle's house forever.

I wasn't thinking bad thoughts about Rochelle when we went outside that day. I hardly knew her. I was just being polite when

I asked for the can. I was trying to teach Rochelle about the kind of sports equipment we use on Burnridge. I was about to toss the can into the trash when Anthony spotted it in my hand. He began yelling, "Kick the can, kick the can!" Kids appeared from nowhere. Bottle caps were pocketed as skelly games were stopped. Marbles were scooped off manhole covers. A double-dutch contest, a stoopball game, a hopscotch match, and at least three games of jacks ended in an instant. Spaldings and yo-yos were stashed as at least fifty Burnridge kids massed at the Firestone stoop.

"Come on, guys," Suzie Q pleaded, "she doesn't know anything. She's just a ignorant yuppie kid."

"An ignorant yuppie kid," corrected Julio.

"So what," everyone else shouted. "She's new on the block and she's *it*."

"You're right. It's the law of the Bronx," said Suzie Q, backing away from Rochelle.

"Life in the Bronx can be tough," said Julio, picking an invisible piece of dust off his shirt.

The kids spread out on the street.

"You're it," I said to Rochelle. I felt responsible and was feeling a little guilty.

"Is it hide-and-seek?" she asked nervously. She had already told me that she was afraid of basements and most other dark places.

"It's kick the can." I explained the game to her: She had to guard the can using only her feet, keeping it from being stolen by the other kids, *and* tag one other kid while the can was in her possession.

"Simple," said Rochelle. "When someone tries to steal the can, I'll tag them. No big deal."

"Hah!" I answered. "If someone else kicks the can while

you're tagging another kid, you're still it. You can take the can along with you by kicking it—like in soccer. But you can't pick it up."

"Easy. Fun," said Rochelle.

"Look, Rochelle, if a kid steals the can from you while you're it, you have to steal it back before you can tag someone." My guilt was fading fast.

"This game is for simpletons." Rochelle put the can on the ground. Guilt totally gone, I took off.

Kick the can is what is done to new kids on Burnridge. There is no way on earth a kid can win against all the kids on a block. Everyone who is outside usually plays—even kids as young as five can join in. If the person leaves the can to tag someone, another kid rushes in and kicks it. Then the other kids bat the can back and forth—keeping it from the person who is it. Kick the can, like ring-a-levio, can go on all day.

The difference is that ring-a-levio, a complicated kind of hide-and-seek, is played with two teams, the larger the better. Kick the can is a neighborhood initiation—one kid against everyone else. Usually we end the game by carrying the new kid—who has collapsed onto the pavement—to the corner, pooling our change and treating him or her to as much pizza or ice cream our money will buy. To be accepted on our block, all a kid has to do is show heart and good humor.

After about fifteen minutes of being it, a very sweaty Rochelle finally realized what the game was all about. Instead of sticking with it, she picked up the dented can and, in an awful snit, stomped into her house.

"She took the can," said one kid.

"That's creepy," said another.

"A real toad," said a third.

"Who gets the pizza?" asked Suzie Q.

"She'll never last," Anthony predicted.

Rochelle's mother slammed out of her front door and hollered to me, "Loretta Bernstein, you are an ill-mannered ingrate. You may never again enter this house. You and your ruffian friends are banned. Forever." She closed the door.

"Did she call us a name?" asked Suzie Q.

"She called Loretta two names, I think," said Calvin.

"I counted a total of three," said Julio.

"What did I do?" I asked.

"You provided the can," said Julio.

"Actually, Rochelle's mother gave it to me," I said.

"Nice going," said Anthony. The streetlights came on and we all raced home.

You have to admit that we are an interesting bunch of kids—even if some of us are obnoxious. That's a word I learned from Julio.

TWO

THE BLOCK

On school days, at exactly 8:35, the elementary-school kids on our block meet on the corner of Burnridge and 112th Avenue. We wait a few minutes for latecomers; then, at about 8:40, we begin walking to P.S. 46. P.S. stands for public school. In the Bronx, we don't have too many fancy names for elementary schools.

At three o'clock we walk home together. This is what is known on Burnridge as the Block Buddy System. Just about everyone over the age of eight has someone to look out for. About half the kids wear whistles on strings. I'm a whistle-wearer, and I take care of Calvin. Suzie Q and I keep an eye out for each other, and we both watch Rochelle—Suzie Q because Rochelle's mother gives her five packages of lunch Twinkies a week, and me because I have no choice: Rochelle sticks to us like a growth. Rochelle is afraid of everything in the Bronx.

I wouldn't mind walking with any other kid on the block—including Vicious Henry. Julio says Vicious Henry is psychotic. That means he's crazy and can't help what he does. Rochelle is not crazy. She's just a pain. So minding her on the way to school is worse than almost anything. She embarrasses me. She walks to school looking like a nervous chicken. Her head darts from side to side as she suspiciously watches every person we pass. She jumps two feet in the air whenever she hears a loud noise, and she makes little frightened peeping noises whenever we go by another group of kids.

All this is bad policy in our part of the Bronx. The way we live here safely is to walk tall, look confident, and develop what Julio calls a quick repartee—a good street rap. On the way to school, I pretend I don't even know the jumpy human bird skipping alongside me. I can't take the chance of spoiling my reputation only a year before I'll be allowed to travel around the neighborhood alone.

Four blocks, three crossings, a couple of abandoned buildings, five rubble-filled lots, a drug dealer or two, and some bad kids lie between our block and the school. With the Buddy System, we get to where we're walking safely. Nobody messes with us—we're organized and united, *and* thirty whistles blown at once can get a whole lot of attention fast. They can also cause a lifetime headache for any perp—that's short for perpetrator, which means criminal.

On Fridays, we usually run home. When we get to the block, most of the kids go to Catarina's Candy Store or Anagnos's Pizza and Greek Specialty Shop, which are across from each

21

other on Burnridge near 112th Street. The rest of us—the kids on the Friday shift—rush home, change into our oldest clothes, and report to work.

A while back, our block was starting to look like many other blocks in poor city neighborhoods. You know, the ones they always show on the news—the ones that look wrecked. What happened to those streets and neighborhoods is what Julio calls "urban deterioration caused by economic greed."

It's simpler than it sounds. Buildings naturally get old. A building that is falling apart is like a car that has been driven a couple of million miles without stopping for a change of oil or a brake job. Just like a car, an old building needs a rest. It needs bodywork. It needs a tune-up. It needs paint. But many landlords want the rents coming in every month, no matter what. Apartments are kept full: One family moves out and another moves in, sometimes on the same day. Since the rents for old apartments in old buildings in poor neighborhoods are not very high, many landlords make a profit by not bothering to fix things when they break. Some don't even bother to buy heating fuel in the winter.

Tenants complain but nothing happens. They can't move to someplace better because they don't have enough money to pay higher rents. The building keeps rotting. The windows break and the heat goes off and the pipes freeze and the plumbing bursts and the ceilings fall down from flooding and the rats that have been living in the crumbling walls move into closets and kitchens. People who are lucky enough to find other apartments they can afford move away. People who aren't stay. Finally, when the building is a complete wreck, the City of New York takes it over. The government becomes the landlord.

My mother says that governments usually make terrible landlords. My father says that by the time the city gets a building, there's not much left to work with. Whatever the case, things usually get worse. The boiler might be fixed by the city but someone forgets to send the plumbers. When the plumbers finally arrive, the roof might be leaking. Paint and plaster peel off ceilings and walls in huge chunks. The remaining tenants lose hope but stay because they have no choice.

One day, an inspector shows up and says the building is unfit for human habitation. It's time to turn it over to the rats and mice and cockroaches. The last tenants are kicked out. Workmen arrive and seal the doors and windows with bricks, boards, and big signs which say NO TRESPASSING and CONDEMNED BUILDING.

But some human beings don't care or can't care what the city says about a building. Soon people begin moving back in. Maybe they're drug addicts or a street gang or a few of the people who used to live in the building and are now homeless. Everything that can be stripped away and sold, like old copper pipes and lighting fixtures, gets ripped out and ripped off. The building becomes a shell—crumbling walls and bare floors. The next thing that usually happens is fire—started by someone trying to stay warm or someone who has been careless with a cigarette butt. After the fire has burned out the floors and stairways, bulldozers come and flatten what's left. That's why we have so many rubble-filled lots in our part of the Bronx.

Most of the Bronx is pretty nice—some of it is beautiful—but blocks and blocks of the Bronx near Burnridge look as if they have been bombed. Our block was starting to look like the rest of the neighborhood. It was awful. The city had already taken over most of the houses. Windows were broken, people froze in the winter, plumbing didn't work. Everyone was depressed. The old people were afraid to stay and afraid to go. They talked

23

about better times on Burnridge that only they could remember. The younger people didn't want to lose lifetime friends, but they wanted to leave. In the end it didn't matter who wanted to stay or go; hardly anybody could afford the rents anywhere else.

One day the city workers came and boarded up the first building to become totally empty between the two 112s. That night, somebody set it on fire. After the fire trucks left, everyone hung around in the street and had a meeting. That's how the Burnridge Neighborhood Association got started.

The Association sent a delegation to City Hall. They went to city council meetings. They talked to the Bronx borough president and the United States congressman from our district. In the end, the City of New York agreed to sell most of the rotten, old buildings on our block to the Neighborhood Association for one dollar each. My father says it was no bargain, because in return, the people in the Association agreed to fix what they now owned, which were all the buildings on the block but two—the one the Firestones bought and the witch's house.

So far, we've fixed up twenty buildings, and that includes one real apartment house with five stories, an elevator, and over thirty apartments. We've also planted trees, and built fences to separate our street from the crumbling buildings and garbage-filled lots on the streets behind us.

Everyone on our block belongs to the Neighborhood Association, including all the kids. Every Neighborhood Association member has a special job to do to make our block nice. The younger kids pick up litter, plant flowers in flower boxes in the spring, and weed around the new trees. Some of the older kids are learning carpentry. Some work at plumbing and painting and floor sanding. The middle kids, like me, help by sweeping up or carrying out debris or sanding old wooden banisters, or running errands. The adults do all the big jobs. Everyone on the block pitches in, doing whatever is needed. Nobody gets paid. Everybody gets a new home sooner or later.

Each time we finish a building, we have a block party to celebrate. Another bunch of rat palaces is gone forever. At the party, the people living in the renovated building sign papers and buy their apartments from the Association for the price of their rent. The deal is that after you get your apartment, you keep working on other apartments. No one is finished until our block is finished. It's called sweat equity. We're trading hard work for homes. We started on the worst places and now, after six years, we're on our last building.

The block is guarded by the Burnridge Neighborhood Watch. Members of the Watch keep loud police whistles by their windows. When one of them spots trouble, he or she leans out and begins blowing as hard as possible. Soon windows fly open all over the block. The noise of the whistles is so loud that you have to cover your ears or get hurt. While this is going on, official phoners begin calling the police. In the meantime, the rest of the neighborhood gets involved. The Bat Squad—men and women who are in good shape and not at work when the alarm is sounded—rush into the street swinging baseball bats over their heads while screaming blood-chilling threats.

Usually, by the time the police arrive, the person causing trouble is surrounded or has run off. The Neighborhood Watch has chased away or caught purse snatchers, muggers, a whole bunch of graffiti artists, and a few stupid thieves who thought they could steal our construction materials. Drug dealers and other neighborhood bad types won't even walk down our block anymore. The word has gotten around the Bronx: If you want to do something that can't be done at high noon in the middle of a crowded street in front of a police station, stay off Burn-ridge between the two 112s.

Mrs. Diaz, founder of the Neighborhood Watch, says the way we protect the block is by "almost nonviolent self-defense." Whatever it is, it works. Our block is a safe place for a kid to play.

Most of the people in the Window Brigade of the Neighborhood Watch are over the age of seventy. They're the ones who are around most of the day. They enjoy looking out their windows in cold weather and sitting in chairs on the stoops and sidewalks when it gets hot. The Window Brigade is a pretty sharp group. They know the name and age of every kid on the block. They watch after us but they also *watch* us. We kids call them the Pane Peepers. When you start a fight or try to grab an apple from the stand in front of Dave's Deli and Grocery or try to sneak around the corner onto one of the 112s, you'll *always* hear someone shouting at you:

"Hey, Charlie, put back that fruit. Don't be a delinquent."

"Oy there, Mikey boy! Stoopball is played against stoops, not glass. If God Himself were living on earth, people would break His window."

"Suzie Q, get off Wanda. Wanda, why did you start a fight? If the head is a fool, the whole body is done for. A good lesson for you."

If the words of wisdom from the Window Brigade don't stop a kid, the Big Threat is used:

"If you don't listen, I'm going to tell your mother."

On our block, there is nothing that stops a kid faster than the Big Threat. There is no way to escape the eyes and ears of the Pane Peepers. Even in our secret places behind the buildings, we've tried—and failed.

Practically all of the buildings on our block are narrow and deep. Around eighty years ago they were built right up next to each other so there are no side windows in any of them. Some buildings have front and rear apartments. Some have long, narrow apartments running the length of the buildings. These are called railroad apartments because they remind people of railroad cars. Each building has an air shaft that runs down its center from the roof to the ground floor. These give the inside rooms a little air and light. It depends on the building. An air shaft is usually small enough so you can open a window and hand your neighbor something—like a cup of sugar or a plate of cookies—or whisper a secret to a friend without leaving your apartment. Lots of conversations take place through windows in the air shafts.

You can basically see three things from an air-shaft window: the bottom of the shaft, the inside of a room in your neighbor's apartment, or, if you lean way out and twist your head, the sky. The only real window views on Burnridge are front and rear— toward the street or what could have been backyards if there had been enough space.

Most of the buildings on our block have stoops. Stoops are wide cement or brick steps leading up to the front door of a building. The top step is wider than the rest—like a little front porch without a roof. Julio says that stoops were invented by the Dutch settlers in New York City. A really good stoop has at least five steps. Stoops are where kids play cards and jacks and stoopball and other games in nice weather and where everyone hangs out to talk on hot nights.

There is only one front yard on our block and no real back-yards. Behind the buildings, covered with cement, are the narrow spaces which might once have been small gardens. These are the alleys of Burnridge Avenue—our favorite places to hang out. When you stand in an alley, you can see from one end of the block to the other. You can imagine you are in a tunnel. Most of the day, the buildings and the fences keep out the sunlight. When you enter an alley, the temperature drops. It feels mysterious. Some of our best adventures have taken place in the alleys of Burnridge.

By using the alleys, a kid can get from 112th Street to 112th Avenue without ever being on the street. There are two ways to get to an alley. One is legal for the kids on Burnridge and one is absolutely forbidden to those of us under eleven. The legal way is to go into a building, go through the ground floor or basement hallway, and out the back door—boring but quick. The illegal way to get to the alleys is to go around the block, cut through one of the empty lots on the next street, and climb a fence. This, of course, means first getting off the block without being spotted from a front window by a Peeper. Then you have to duck into an empty lot and make it back into our alley without being seen from a rear window. This is not easy. Usually kids only do the Alley Sneak on a dare.

Suzie Q was once caught leaving and returning by the oldest member of the Window Brigade, Mrs. Gold. Mrs. Gold is ninety-two. She had front window-watch duty that afternoon. She watched Suzie Q sneak around the corner, suspected what was up, grabbed her camera, left her apartment, and went into the Petersons' apartment, which has rear windows. There Mrs. Gold waited for the right moment before taking a Polaroid shot of Suzie Q getting stuck between two loose boards as she tried to squeeze through a hole she had created in the fence. Suzie Q was punished for leaving the block and for destroying Neighborhood Association property. She didn't get an allowance for three months.

The alleys pretty much belong to the kids and the supers and

28

the cats of Burnridge Avenue. There are four professional building superintendents on our block. We call them supers. They
take care of the buildings—keeping halls clean, making repairs,
shoveling sidewalks when it snows, and taking the garbage cans
from the alleys to the street and back again on garbage pickup
days. On other days, the supers check to make sure no garbage
has spilled out of the cans onto the ground. But they don't
spend much time in the alleys. The only other adults who use
the alleys go there to stuff their garbage into the metal cans or
leave food for the cats. Their average stay is under a minute.

The cats spend the most time in the alleys. No dogs can get
back there, so the cats are free to visit each other and hunt the
rats and mice which try to raid the garbage cans. Some of the
cats belong to people on the block and some are strays. Most
people on the block like cats. Even those who don't like them
a whole lot respect them for what they do to the rodents who
keep trying to move back into our buildings.

That's why nobody ever expected the cats of Burnridge to
begin disappearing.

THREE

THE DOCTOR IS MISSING

"The Doctor is gone," said Suzie Q.

"What do you mean by *gone?*" I asked.

"Gone. Nowhere to be found. Missing. He hasn't been seen anywhere for three days." Suzie Q was very upset.

The Doctor is a huge, silver-gray tomcat. He is everybody's favorite alley cat. Even people who don't ordinarily like cats like The Doctor. Most everyone on Burnridge has tried to get The Doctor to be a pet by inviting him in and bribing him with chicken livers or tuna fish or chunks of hamburger. The Doctor is always a gentleman. He eats his meal, says his thanks, takes a nap, and asks to be let out. The Doctor is his own cat.

In cold weather, just before the streetlights go on, The Doctor appears on the sidewalk, picks some happy kid, and demands to be carried to the kid's home. There is no way you can force The Doctor to choose you. There is no way you can get him to go to the same apartment two nights in a row. No matter where he spends the night, The Doctor behaves according to his own rules. After eating, he offers a dignified amount of affection, finds the softest place in the warmest corner, and goes to sleep. If you're lucky, that place is the foot of your bed. Having The Doctor actually spend the night on your bed is considered better than finding a bagful of four-leaf clovers. In the morning, The Doctor goes back to the alleys to visit his cats. He is the king of the cats of Burnridge Avenue.

No one knows how old The Doctor is. Mr. Jones gave him his name as a sign of respect when The Doctor showed up on Burnridge Avenue seven years ago. Mr. Jones says that The Doctor is a Doctor of Catology—a world-class expert in all things feline. No one has ever seen him fight with another cat but there is no question that he is boss. The meanest, toughest, wildest cats on the block turn into sweet pussycats when The Doctor is around.

"Maybe he's just staying with someone," I said to Suzie Q.

"The Doctor doesn't do sleep-overs until the nights get cold—and they aren't yet. Besides, it's daytime now." Suzie Q's voice was squeaking with tension.

"Maybe he's sick and someone's taking care of him," said Calvin.

"I would have heard," said Anthony.

"Maybe he got himself locked in a basement," said Julio.

We searched every basement on Burnridge. We rang doorbells, talked to every kid we could find, and questioned every member of the Window Brigade. Nobody had seen The Doctor for days. The entire block was on alert. We were so desperate, we considered actually talking to the witch of Burnridge, who happened to be walking up the street dragging a shopping cart loaded with grocery bags.

"Ask her," said Suzie Q.

"You ask her," I answered.

"What's the big deal?" Rochelle smiled her superior smile.

"You're afraid of everything else in the Bronx—how come you're not afraid of the witch?" said Anthony.

"There are no witches. She's just an old lady." Rochelle had used her prissy know-it-all voice.

"Then you ask her," demanded Anthony.

Rochelle took a few steps toward the witch. The witch stopped, covered the lower part of her face with her black shawl, and turned to Rochelle. Rochelle bolted. She just took off and didn't stop running until she was on her own stoop.

"Heh. Heh. Heh," cackled the witch. She looked Anthony right in the eye and winked. "Little boy, want to help an old lady home with her bundles?" The witch's voice sounded a thousand years old.

Anthony nodded, grabbed the handle of the shopping cart, and dragged it down the block. The witch tottered along beside him. He was back in under five minutes.

"She called you little boy." Suzie Q laughed for the first time that day.

"I guess she can call me anything she wants," said Anthony, not looking upset at all.

"I thought you were a goner," I said.

"What did she say?" asked Julio.

"Nothing," said Anthony.

"To you? Not possible," insisted Julio.

"Did you ask her about The Doctor?" I said.

Anthony glared at me. "No, we discussed the price of fish in Borneo."

"You don't have to get nasty," I said.

Anthony gave me his most brilliant smile.

"You're hiding something, Anthony DeRosa," I accused.

"Let's get back to the Doctor hunt. We're wasting time." Suzie Q was shifting from foot to foot impatiently.

"Who's going to check Maury's Poultry and Meat Emporium?" asked The Raven.

"We already looked behind the store," said Julio. "Three cats were eating scraps. The Doctor wasn't there."

"Not behind. *In*," said The Raven.

"In? Why?" I asked.

"He makes sausages in there," said The Raven. "Have you ever seen the meat hanging in his freezer? Can't tell what it once was."

Julio looked as if he might throw up, except Julio never did anything that messy.

"You've been reading too many of Mr. Poe's horrible stories," said Rochelle, who had returned as soon as the witch had walked away.

"They're not horrible," said The Raven. "They're works of art. The man was a Bronx genius."

"The man was a Bronx sick-o," said Rochelle.

The Raven backed his wheelchair over Rochelle's foot.

"Ouch!" she screamed, hopping around.

"Sorry," said The Raven, grinning.

"Don't mess with my man's main man," said Calvin, defending Edgar Allan Poe.

"Ever read one of his horror stories—if you can read, shrimp?" said Rochelle.

"Don't pick on my brother." I was ready to fight.

"Stop it!" shouted Suzie Q. "The only thing that counts is that The Doctor is missing."

I had never seen Suzie Q avoid an argument, especially one where she could earn brownies for defending Rochelle. I had never realized how much she admired The Doctor.

"We've looked everywhere," Rochelle whined. "What does it matter anyway. He's only an old, beat-up alley cat." In the next moment, Rochelle was lying on the sidewalk and Suzie Q was kneeling on her back.

"Take it back, yuppie scum!" Suzie Q grabbed a sizable handful of Rochelle's hair and began pulling.

"Mommy!" screamed Rochelle.

"So much for nonviolence," said Julio.

"Get off that child, Susan Quinn. You're not on Saturday-night wrestling." The Window Brigade was on the job.

"Get off her, Suzie Q," I begged. "If your mother hears about this, she'll lock you in and you won't be able to help find The Doctor."

Suzie Q stood up. "Maybe he was catnapped," she said.

"Who would bother to steal an old, rotten cat?" said Rochelle, staggering to her feet and rubbing the back of her head.

"Watch your mouth, rat-face," warned Suzie Q.

"Maybe he was run over by a car," whispered Calvin.

"Eat your tongue," said Suzie Q.

"Someone would have found his body. He never leaves the block," said The Raven. We forced ourselves to look under all the parked cars. For a few minutes we were happy not to see The Doctor.

"Maybe he was cooked for dinner by some horrible, smelly homeless people," Rochelle suggested.

Suzie Q's hands were reaching for Rochelle's neck when I

stepped between them. "You're all heart, Shelly. People around here don't eat cats—not even hungry, homeless people."

"This conversation is making me queasy," said Julio.

"What does that mean?" asked Calvin.

"I think Julio is threatening to throw up," I said.

"No way," said The Raven.

Days went by. People left dishes of The Doctor's favorite foods on stoops and in the alleys. After school, kids wandered around calling his name. At the end of a week, we all gave up. With no Doctor around to make peace, the Burnridge cats began choosing a new leader. The yowls and screeches we heard at night reminded us that the best cat any of us had ever known was gone. It was a sad time on Burnridge Avenue.

FOUR

CATASTROPHE

"Orange Cat is missing," Calvin announced. It was a Friday.
We had all changed into our after-school clothes, and I was
headed for work. It was my turn to run errands for the reno-
vation crew. Naturally, Calvin was with me.

"Who told you?" I asked.

"No one. I saw for myself. She's my cat."

"Orange Cat is feral," I said, using a word Julio had taught
me.

"No she's not. What's *feral?*" asked Calvin.

"Wild. A wild animal descended from tame stock. Or an
animal who became wild from a state of domestication. Un-

tamed. Existing in a state of nature. Savage." Julio had joined us.

"I could have told him that," I complained.

"Not as well," said Julio.

"I didn't understand anything you said, Julio—except the part about being wild. I'm only seven."

"But a very sharp seven," said Julio. "Stick with me and by the time you're ten, you'll be a fountain of knowledge, a genius, a walking encyclopedia, a—"

"You're wrong," said Calvin.

"Don't underestimate yourself, Calvin," said Julio.

"Under what?" said Calvin. Before Julio could answer, Calvin went on, "Loretta's wrong about Orange Cat. She isn't wild. Feral. She's my friend. I've been feeding her for weeks. She even slept on my bed a couple of nights—I snuck her in."

"No way. Orange Cat, the Terror of Burnridge, the cat no human hand has ever touched? Stop telling stories, Calvin."

"I'm not. It's the truth. I touch her. She likes me. She just doesn't like other cats much."

"And how about her attitude toward people?" I asked suspiciously.

"Nobody ever took the time to like her before. I was going to ask Mom if Orange could be my pet and live in my room all of the time, and now it's too late." Calvin was crying.

"He tamed her," said Julio. "Remarkable, especially considering he did it behind your back when you were supposed to be minding him, Loretta."

"You believe Calvin?"

"Most certainly. Why would he invent a story about a chewed-up, unappealing feline such as Orange Cat?"

"Machismo," I suggested. "The kid who tamed Orange Cat would have the beginning of a reputation."

"Look at him, Loretta. He's a wreck," Julio had his arm around the shoulder of the sobbing Calvin.

"Okay. Okay. Orange Cat is Calvin's pet. I believe you. Stop crying. We'll look for him."

"Her," Calvin corrected me, and blew his nose.

Most of my friends were working that day—getting coffee and soft drinks for the crew. When we were finished, we went on another cat hunt. Once again, we had no luck. The search for Orange Cat brought back all our sad feelings about The Doctor.

Since it was a Friday and the weather was still mild, we were allowed to go outside after dinner. We would be allowed to stay there until eight-thirty. We met on the stoop of Rochelle's house.

Rochelle's house is the only house on the block owned by a single family. The Firestones call their house a brownstone, which makes the place sound like it belongs on some rich block in Manhattan. Julio says that brownstone is a brown sandstone they used to use for building houses in New York City. He says that brownstone is also what people call any four- or five-story row house in the city, even if it's made of brick. Since the Firestones' house is a three-story brick building, the whole thing seems beside the point to me.

We like meeting on the Firestone stoop because, as Julio says, "Rochelle's mother feels obligated to entertain us in a civilized manner. She considers us barbarians who need to be tamed." We don't care what her reasons are as long as she keeps bringing soda and chips out to the stoop whenever we are around. No neighborhood adults ever hang out in front of the Firestone house. As always, the stoop was ours that evening.

"Your mother gives us food out here so we won't think about going inside," said The Raven.

"That's not true," said Rochelle.

"Then let's meet inside tonight," said The Raven, sliding out of his wheelchair and onto the second step of the stoop. He had lifted himself to the top of the stoop when Suzie Q stepped in.

"Stop teasing her, Raven. It's not her fault her mother is a snot."

Rochelle handed Suzie Q a candy bar.

"Bribery really works," said The Raven.

"Can it," warned Suzie Q.

"Watch how you talk to The Raven," growled The Raven.

"What about Orange Cat," whined Calvin.

"Yeah, stick to what we're here for," I said. Calvin isn't my favorite person in the world, but he is my brother. I felt sorry for him that day. Besides, I knew we had a serious problem on our hands.

"Did you guys notice anything else when we were looking for Orange?" I asked.

"Like what?" said Suzie Q.

"Like, a bunch of cats are missing from the block."

"Like who?" asked The Raven.

"Like Anthony, Snubnose, Sweet Blossom the Kitten, and Charlotte," I said.

"Someone mention me?" Anthony had arrived. He grabbed a soda.

"Have a soda, Anthony," I said.

"Don't mind if I do. What were you saying about me?"

"We were talking about your namesake, Anthony the Cat," said Julio.

"Tony Tomcat," said Anthony. "He's missing."

"You know already," said Suzie Q.

"Of course I know. Orange Cat, Snubnose, Sweet Blossom the Kitten, and a bunch of other cats are also missing. And garbage cans have been raided behind a number of buildings during the past week."

"What do garbage cans have to do with cats?" I asked.

"Nothing. I just thought you'd like to know."

"Know what? You have something on your mind. Tell us."

"Two families from 2790 are missing old cats who are afraid of the street and have never in their lives gone farther than a fire escape."

"This is getting spooky," said Suzie Q.

"You changed the subject again, Anthony," I accused.

"Stick to what's important, Loretta," said Julio.

"The cats aren't on the street," said Suzie Q.

"Or in the alleys."

"Or the basements."

"Maybe they wandered off the block onto one of the 112s," Anthony suggested.

"That would only make sense if one cat were missing," said Julio. "What we're now talking about are cats who had never before left home. We appear to have a mysterious epidemic of disappearing cats."

"Maybe a cat-hater is poisoning them," suggested Rochelle.

"You have rotten ideas, Shelly."

"Don't call me Shelly."

"Stick to the point. Nobody really *hates* cats on this block, do they, Anthony?" asked The Raven.

"My father does," said Rochelle. "Wild ones, at any rate. He says they smell up our patio and make too much noise at night." Then she clamped her hand over her mouth and looked sorry she had said anything.

"What's a patio?" asked Calvin.

"In this case it's an alley with some metal furniture in it," said Julio.

We were all staring at Rochelle, who had practically admitted that her father had poisoned our cats. She started squirming.

"But he would never *kill* an animal," she shouted. "*Never!* He gives money to Save the Whales . . . and the National Wildlife Association . . . and—"

"Cats aren't whales or bears or wolves," said Julio. We put our sodas down and started moving off the Firestone stoop. Even Suzie Q was backing away from Rochelle.

"Look, we have a pet cat. My dad likes some cats. He just doesn't like stray cats very much. But he would *never* hurt anything. I told you, some stranger must be getting rid of the cats."

"Right—some hungry homeless person. Well, Shelly, there haven't been any strangers skulking around the neighborhood. Ask Anthony." Julio was now standing at the curb.

"Wait a second. Let's try to be fair. You really have a cat, Shelly?" I asked. "How come we never see it?"

"She stays inside, and my name is Rochelle," said Rochelle.

"How come nobody ever sees it at a window? All housecats look out windows," said Calvin, who, for a little kid, was sounding pretty smart.

"Because my mother doesn't let her in the living room or the master bedroom or the guest room. Those are the rooms facing front."

"What's a master bedroom?" asked Calvin.

"The biggest bedroom—where the master sleeps," said Julio.

"Like when there were slaves?" asked Calvin.

"Prove it," said Suzie Q.

"Prove what?" Rochelle was getting confused. So was I, to tell the truth.

"Save your vocabulary questions for later, Calvin," I ordered. "And stop answering him, Julio."

Julio ignored me. "A master is a person who rules, governs, or directs—a person in charge. There were slave masters and . . ."

"Shut up, Julio!" Suzie Q clenched her fist. Julio stopped talking. Suzie Q turned to Rochelle. "Okay, rat-bait, prove you have a cat. Bring her out and show us."

"Okay," said Rochelle.

We settled back onto the stoop. We must have been waiting for ten minutes when a horrible scream came from inside the Firestone house. The front door opened, and Rochelle and Mr. and Mrs. Firestone rushed out.

"She's gone! Champion Princess Ponga, the Jewel of Siam, is gone." Rochelle and her mother were crying. Mr. Firestone looked bugged.

"Which one of you unlatched her cage door?" he demanded.

"What cage?" I whispered to Julio.

"Princess Ponga has a big exercise cage on the patio where she can go to get fresh air. There's a cat door leading from it to the house and an outside cage door we keep shut tight and locked so she can't escape," explained Rochelle.

"I thought that was a strange-looking pigeon coop," said Anthony.

"Just as I suspected." Mr. Firestone glared at Anthony. "I should have called the police the second time I found the lid off the garbage can and half our garbage missing. You kids have been mucking around on my patio. Which one of you took her?"

"None of us took your cat. We've seen the cage because the alleys are our turf," said The Raven.

"That patio is *my* turf, mister. That's why I put a fence around it," said Mr. Firestone.

"Fences can be gotten over, under, or through," said The Raven. "Especially by an escaped cat. We didn't unlock the stupid cage door. We didn't steal your stupid cat. It's not our thing. Besides, we didn't even know you had a cat."

"And not a single one of us has any interest in your garbage!" Julio sounded totally disgusted.

"Princess whatever isn't the only cat around here who's missing," said Anthony.

"Missing?" said Mr. Firestone.

"Gone, daddy," said Rochelle. "Not to be found anywhere."

"Nonsense. I'll pay you a dollar each to search the alleys and basements for Princess," said Mrs. Firestone.

"Okay, Mrs. Firestone," said Julio.

"You can't take money for a cat search," I said.

"Why not? I've got a cash-flow problem," said Julio.

"What's that?" asked Calvin.

"I'm broke," said Julio.

"Oh. Me too. What do we do, Loretta? We just looked everywhere," said Calvin.

"That was before dinner. Let's try again," I said.

"But it's almost dark. What will we be able to see?" said Calvin.

"Good point, smart kid," said Julio. "You got any flashlights, Mrs. Firestone?"

With the help of the flashlights and the Firestones, and a whole lot of other kids who knew an easy dollar when they saw one, we searched for the missing Champion Princess Ponga, the Jewel of Siam. Wherever she was, whatever she was, she wasn't on our block.

"Well," said Anthony as we walked up the stairs to our apartments, "she may be missing, but she sure is missing in good company."

"I want Orange Cat back," said Calvin.

"And The Doctor," I added.

"And Snubnose and Sweet Blossom the Kitten and Charlotte—and Tony Tomcat," said Anthony.

"Julio said this is a catastrophe," I said.

"What's that?" asked Calvin.

"A great disaster. A terrible misfortune," I explained to my little brother.

"Maybe not," said Anthony.

"What do you mean? Do you know something?" I asked.

"I have an idea."

"What is it?" I asked.

"See you tomorrow," said Anthony, and headed upstairs.

"Sometimes you make me mad enough to bite," I called after him, and slammed our apartment door.

FIVE

CONFUSION ON BURNRIDGE

Saturday is the major errand and chore day on Burnridge. Nobody sleeps late because there's just too much to do. So when I walked out onto our stoop at eight-thirty the next morning, I expected to see my neighbors going about their business. What I saw instead was a near riot.

The street was packed with kids—hundreds of them. They were climbing up firescapes and peering into windows. They were hanging off rooftops. They were crawling under cars. They were sneaking into basements. They were running in and out of stores. They were shoving and pushing each other. They were making catlike noises or calling, "Here Princess," or

"Here, kitty, come here kitty," in high-pitched, squeaky voices. Some of the kids were carrying cans of cat food, others little balls of wool attached to string. A few had cat toys clutched in their hands. Two were sprinkling catnip on the sidewalk in a trail which led to a small cage, and two others were trying to snag anything that moved with what looked like long-handled fishing nets.

Every few minutes a kid would pounce and come up with an animal tightly held in his or her arms. The kid would then scream, "I've found her!" and begin rushing toward the Firestone house. I saw Tabbycat Meatball, the oldest, fattest cat on the block—a cat who never went past her window sill—captured and deposited in Mr. Firestone's arms four times by four different kids. Each time Mr. Firestone put her down, Tabby would try waddling home. About halfway there, some other kid would grab her. Finally, Mrs. Goldblum, her owner, went to the rescue.

"Cat robbers!" she yelled at everyone as she staggered down the street carrying her heavy pet. "Thievers! Vandals! Stay off my building! The next person who climbs my firescape and lays a finger on my cat winds up in jail!" Nobody paid any attention to her.

Those who weren't cat hunting were watching Mrs. Washington running after a kid, pounding him on the head with a rolled-up newspaper. He was racing toward the Firestone house with Mrs. Washington's miniature schnauzer, Fritz, in his arms.

"Leave me alone, lady," he yelled as he ran. "I ain't sharing the reward. I found the cat, not you."

"Idiot, that's my dog. Let him go," Mrs. Washington gasped as she landed a solid blow to his shoulder.

"Ouch! This here is no dog, lady. You're not going to trick

me!" The boy ran up the Firestone stoop, pushed aside a crowd of grown-ups, and practically threw Fritz at Mr. Firestone.

"Gimme the hundred bucks!" he demanded.

Fritz bit Mr. Firestone on the thumb. Mrs. Washington gave the boy one last hit with the newspaper and retrieved Fritz. The boy went back to cat hunting.

"What's going on?" I asked Suzie Q, who rushed by, not noticing me.

She didn't answer, so I ran after her and grabbed her arm. "Stop!" I shouted in her ear.

"Bug off, bozo," she said. I held on tight as Suzie Q dragged me down the block.

"Suzie Q, it's me, Loretta, your lifelong friend."

"Get off me or I'll punch your face out!" she snarled, shaking her arm.

"Suzie Q, it's me. *Look at me!*" I pleaded.

Suzie Q stopped. Her face was red. She was sweating and breathing hard. She looked as if she had been running in a race.

"Oh, it's you, Loretta. I thought it was one of those rotten, turf-busting invaders," she gasped.

"Turf-busting invaders?" I asked. "What are you talking about?"

"Look!" shouted Suzie Q, pointing to a poster tacked to a utility pole.

$100 REWARD
NO QUESTIONS ASKED

FOR THE RETURN OR INFORMATION LEADING TO THE RETURN OF
CHAMPION PRINCESS PONGA, THE JEWEL OF SIAM.
SIAMESE CAT
CREAM-COLORED BODY, DARK BROWN MARKINGS

LAST SEEN WEARING RED LEATHER
COLLAR WITH RHINESTONE TRIM.

RETURN to 2745 BURNRIDGE AVENUE
or CALL 555-6099

"One hundred dollars?" I said. "Are they serious? That's a fortune!"

"Yeah. Serious and stupid. The Firestones made a zillion of these posters last night and nailed them all over the neighborhood. Kids are here from everywhere—even from across the Grand Concourse." Suzie Q's face got redder.

"Chill out, Suzie Q. You're going to faint or something."

"Who cares. One of the invaders is going to find that stupid Princess and get the reward."

"What invaders?" I asked.

"Those invaders." Suzie Q swung her arm in a big circle. A new group of kids arrived at a run from around a corner. I didn't recognize any of them.

"Strangers. Robbers. Sneaks," muttered Suzie Q.

Rochelle pushed her way through the growing crowd and came up to us. "Why aren't you looking for Princess?" she complained.

"Shut up, dumb-mouth," said Suzie Q.

Rochelle pulled a fudge brownie from her pocket and handed it to Suzie Q. Suzie Q wouldn't take it.

"I don't think Suzie Q takes bribes from collaborators." Julio had made his way to us.

"What's a collaborator?" asked Calvin. To reach us, he had climbed over three kids who were crawling on the sidewalk making mouselike noises. They hadn't even noticed him.

"Mommy says you have to mind me this morning, Loretta. What's a collaborator?"

48

"A collaborator is a person who cooperates with the enemy," said Julio.

"What enemy?" asked Rochelle.

"Your parents. The invaders," growled Suzie Q.

"Suzie Q is afraid one of these other kids is going to find Princess and get the reward," I said.

"I'm never afraid. I'm bugged," said Suzie Q.

"No cat in its right mind would hang around in the middle of this mess if it could help it," I said.

"Exactly," said Julio. "If the feline is still on the block, she won't be out here waiting to be netted by a maniac making mouse squeaks."

"Maybe Princess is in her wrong mind," said Calvin.

"Don't you dare call Princess crazy," yelled Rochelle.

"I didn't," said Calvin.

"You did," shouted Rochelle.

"SHUT UP," yelled Suzie Q.

"Let's go to the alleys," I suggested. "It's a better place for a cat to hide."

"Am I invited?" asked The Raven.

"We didn't hear you arrive," said Julio.

"Well-oiled wheels are always an advantage," said The Raven.

We had been helping The Raven get his wheelchair into unexpected places for practically our entire lives. So it only took a couple of minutes for us to find the basement we wanted, negotiate the stairs, and wind up in an alley.

"I told you so," growled Suzie Q. "ANTS! COCK-ROACHES! RATS! INVADERS!" she screamed into the sky.

"Invaders. Invaders. Invaders." Her voice echoed off the building walls.

For a moment, all movement froze, like in a photograph.

Then it began again. Kids were everywhere. They were on the fire escapes. They were swarming over the barrier fence. They were overturning garbage cans and running in and out of basements. Those up on the fire escapes were getting tangled in the clotheslines strung between windows and the utility poles across the alley. Clean sheets and towels and underwear drifted through the air to the dirty ground below.

"This is great," giggled Calvin.

"No it isn't, pea brain," said Suzie Q, slapping him on the arm.

"Don't hit my little brother." I stepped between Suzie Q and Calvin.

"Who's going to stop me, bean pole?" she asked, shaking her fist in my face.

"They do look a lot like insects on a rampage," said Julio.

"Susan Quinn, you are on report!" The very loud voice of Mrs. Briggs, vice chairman of the Neighborhood Watch, stopped Suzie Q midpunch.

"Why don't you do something about these invaders, Mrs. Briggs? They're ruining the block. I'm innocent," shouted Suzie Q, unclenching her fist.

"Hah! Ridiculous! Besides, I know your parents. I don't know theirs. We've called the police. Take my advice. Go home. Watch television. Eat apples. Wait until all this blows over." Mrs. Briggs hauled in what remained of her clean laundry and slammed down her window.

"What now?" I asked.

"We lay low until after the police get here," said The Raven.

"Where?" asked Suzie Q.

"My house will be okay," I said.

"No it won't. Mom said company's coming tonight. She doesn't want a mess," said Calvin.

"My baby brother is sick," said Suzie Q.

"My folks are waxing the floors today," said Julio.

"Let's go sit on my stoop," I said.

"When the police come, we can duck inside while they round up the invaders," said Suzie Q.

"What about the apples?" asked Calvin.

"What apples?"

"Mrs. Briggs said we should eat apples. I'm hungry."

"Where's Rochelle? I'm hungry, too," said Suzie Q.

"Let's go sit on the Firestone stoop," said Julio.

We went back through the basement and up onto the street. About half the adults in the neighborhood were in front of the Firestone house, hollering and waving their fists. Mr. Firestone was facing them, trying to make himself heard. Using Raven's wheelchair as a battering ram, we made it through the crush and up to the three top steps. Nobody paid any attention to us.

"You're an idiot, Firestone," shouted a neighbor.

"Who offers a hundred bucks for a cat in this neighborhood?" hollered another.

"Kids from all over the Bronx are crawling in and out of our buildings!"

"Some yutz tried to grab the parrot cage from my window. My *parrot*! They're so crazy that they can't tell a parrot from a cat."

"How about my iguana?" someone asked.

"They took a lizard?"

"And three dogs and every cat that wasn't smart enough to lock itself in a closet," said someone else.

"Maybe it has gotten a little out of hand," said Mr. Firestone. None of the animals were hurt, were they?" he asked.

"That isn't the point, Firestone. Take down those posters. Tell them the reward is off."

"Yeah, take down the posters!" Everyone was shouting at once.

"I can't do that. It would be unfair. A fraud. Besides, they'd destroy my house."

"If you don't do something, we're going to destroy *you*." The crowd of neighbors was getting ugly.

"Should we get out of here?" I asked.

"They won't hurt us," said Julio.

"I'm hungry," Calvin sighed.

The door to the Firestone house opened about a foot. A skinny arm tossed a bag of pretzels and a bag of corn chips to us. The arm disappeared and the door slammed.

"I guess she's afraid to come out," said Suzie Q. "I wonder if she'll bring us some soda." The door opened and closed again with lightning speed. When we turned to look, we saw a six-pack of soda waiting for us.

"She sure can move fast when she wants to," said Suzie Q, opening a can.

Then we heard the sirens. Police cars raced onto Burnridge. One screeched to a stop in front of the Firestone house. Two pulled around and blocked the ends of the street. The rest spread out in between.

"Impressive," said Julio.

"Just like on TV," said Calvin.

"What's going on here?" demanded a very large police sergeant.

All the adults spoke at once. It took a few minutes but the sergeant finally understood. He looked disgusted. He returned to his car and took out a bullhorn.

"ALL CAT HUNTERS WHO DO NOT LIVE ON THIS BLOCK WILL CEASE AND DESIST IMMEDIATELY. GO

HOME. GET OFF THE BUILDINGS. GET OUT OF THE BUILDINGS. GET OFF YOUR BELLIES AND OUT FROM UNDER THE CARS. GO HOME OR YOU'RE UNDER ARREST." He repeated the message in Spanish. He sent two patrolmen with bullhorns behind the buildings to make the same announcement.

It took at least half an hour to herd everyone off the block, out of the alleyways and basements. A number of kids had to be convinced that going to jail was worse than not finding the one-hundred-dollar Princess. There were other kids who had to be convinced that The Jewel of Siam was the cat and not a diamond collar she was wearing. Apparently some of the kids had been planning on keeping "the jewels."

After the block was clear, the sergeant asked Mr. Firestone some questions before instructing his officers. They drove away, but he stayed, drumming his fingers on the handrail of the stoop. After a while, the patrol cars began returning. Each policeman gave the sergeant a pile of posters. When the last policeman had returned, the sergeant spoke.

"Is this all of them, Firestone?" he asked.

Mr. Firestone counted the posters. "Yes."

"Never, never, *never* again pull such a fool stunt in my precinct or I'll run you in for inciting a riot!" The sergeant grabbed the posters from Mr. Firestone and ripped them into small pieces. As he walked to his car we could hear him mumbling to himself, "A cat, a stupid cat. Princess Ponga my eye."

The patrol cars drove away. Everyone except the Firestones applauded and cheered. Burnridge Avenue was back to normal.

"We'll never find Princess now." Rochelle had finally come outside.

"Wrong," I said. "Now we *will* be able to find her."

"Hah!" said Suzie Q. "The cat has probably been chased back to Siam."

"Siam is now Thailand," said Julio.

"Big deal," said Suzie Q.

"Where's Thailand?" asked Calvin.

"Halfway around the world," said Anthony.

"Well, I bet by now she's made it to Manhattan." Suzie Q was rubbing her forehead with her fingers.

"Or she's closer to home—like somewhere in the Bronx," Anthony offered.

"The Bronx is almost forty square miles," said The Raven. "The cat and the hundred-dollar reward are lost forever."

"I don't think so," I said.

"Me either," said Julio.

Julio and I were both staring at a place down the block.

"What do you mean?" asked Rochelle.

"Yeah, what do you mean? There isn't an inch of this block that hasn't been searched," said The Raven.

"There's more than an inch," I said.

"Way more," said Julio.

"That's where they must all be, don't you think?" I asked Julio.

"You are right on the mark, Loretta," he said.

"Where?" everyone asked.

"Right in front of our noses," I said, pointing. "There."

"Oh."

"Oh, no."

"No way."

"Never."

"We're geniuses, Loretta," said Julio.

"You're wrong," said Suzie Q.

"We're not," I said.

"Not geniuses?" asked Calvin.

"Not wrong," I answered.

We sat and stared at the only place no one had dared to look—at the place where we were sure the cats of Burnridge had met an unknown fate.

SIX

THE WITCH'S HOUSE

"LUNCH! 'ALGHADHAA'! ALMUERZO! COME AND GET IT! CHAKULA CHA MCHANA! IL PRANZO! FOOD IS ON! CHUSHOKU! KUMT ESSEN! TIME TO EAT! AH-BYEHD! BRUNCH!" It was noon. Windows were opened all over the block and kids were being summoned home. The call to mealtime on Burnridge always sounds like a meeting of the United Nations is about to take place.

"We can meet after lunch," I said.

"Except Shelly," said Anthony.

"Why can't I meet you and my name is Rochelle."

"Because you'll be eating brunch, not lunch."

"It's the same thing," insisted Rochelle.

"Do you eat brunch at school?" asked Calvin.

"You know I eat lunch with the rest of you," said Rochelle.

"So it isn't the same thing." Calvin was grinning. "That means you can't meet us after lunch."

This conversation had taken place before. It was guaranteed to drive Rochelle crazy.

"I think we're having a language problem, Shell. It must be related to your position as a pioneer on the block. It's difficult to communicate with us natives." Julio smoothed his shirt and headed home.

"My name isn't Shell either and stop picking on me!" Rochelle looked around for Suzie Q but Suzie Q had left at the first sounds of windows opening. Suzie Q has never been late for a meal.

"So we'll meet in front of the big tree," I said.

"Do we have to?" asked Calvin.

"Do you want Orange Cat back?" I asked.

By one o'clock, we were all standing under the enormous tree with the metal sign screwed into its bark: THE OLDEST OAK TREE IN THE BRONX. CIRCA 1700.

The oak tree was part of Bronx history. It was so large that ten kids holding hands could just about circle it. The oak took up most of the space in the one real front yard on Burnridge Avenue. The yard belonged to the farmhouse. The farmhouse and the tree had been there when the Bronx was a wilderness, when instead of sidewalks and cars and buildings there had been forests and fields and streams and deer and bear.

The farmhouse was where the witch lived. No kid in the entire neighborhood had to be warned to stay away from it. We were too scared to go beyond the tree. Even on Halloween, the worst kids in the Bronx knew better than to do any kind of mischief on the farmhouse property—not garbage dumping, not window breaking, not graffiti. During the cat hunt, even kids from across the Grand Concourse didn't trespass. As far as I knew, except for Anthony carrying groceries to the witch's porch, no kid had been within twenty feet of the house for years.

We leaned on the tree and stared at our feet.

"Now what?" asked Anthony.

"Why don't we just ring the doorbell and ask if she's seen Princess," Rochelle suggested in her prissy, know-it-all voice.

"She? You mean the witch?" asked Calvin.

"You must be crazy, Rochelle," said Julio.

"There is no doorbell," said Anthony.

"Then bang on the door with your fist." Rochelle stamped her foot.

"What would be the point? Witches don't give kids straight answers." Anthony was smiling.

"And witches make kids into gingerbread men." Calvin looked petrified.

"Witches? Witches? You're all nuts. Witches are not real. It's just a very old woman who lives here," said Rochelle.

"For almost three hundred years?" I asked.

"What three hundred years?" asked Rochelle.

"She's lived here for almost three hundred years. No one—ever—has seen anyone else move in or out. It's always been the same old woman—same *old* woman—get it? She lived in the farmhouse when it was in a wilderness, when it was on the edge of a town, when it was part of a town, and when, as a house in the Bronx, the Bronx joined New York City in 1898 as a borough." I had been studying Bronx history in school.

"That's ridiculous. You're all chicken. She looks like a regular old lady to me," insisted Rochelle.

"Then why did you run away from her yesterday?" I asked.

"I didn't," said Rochelle.

"You sure did. You were out of sight before any of us could blink our eyes," said Anthony.

"I had to go to the—you know," said Rochelle.

"What's a youknow?" asked Calvin innocently.

"Come on, Rochelle, you stood on your stoop and waited for the witch to leave. Besides, if you're so sure she's a regular person, you go knock on her door. We'll wait here for you—as back-up support," said The Raven.

"She doesn't go out much, so she probably doesn't know anything about Princess." Rochelle was stalling.

"You're stalling," I said.

"What are you afraid of?" asked Suzie Q, who did not like to be thought of as being chicken, even as a member of a larger group. "She's an innocent, harmless, little old lady. There's no such thing as a witch, right?"

"Right!" said Rochelle. "Superstitious peasants," she mumbled, just loud enough for us to hear, as she took two small steps toward the farmhouse. She stopped, bent down, and pretended to pull up her socks. The rest of us leaned against the tree and watched.

"Maybe she's not home," said Rochelle, looking back at us.

"Only way to find out is to knock," said Anthony.

"Or shout for her, Shelly. 'Hey, witch, stick your head out the window and tell me if you have my cat.' "

Rochelle ignored my suggestion and pretended to get interested in a weed that was growing next to a tree root.

Julio, who had been staring at the house and ignoring us, finally spoke. "The witch has been on the street more than usual these past couple of weeks, hasn't she?"

"Always dragging those loaded shopping carts from the big market," said Anthony.

59

"Notice what was in the bags when you carried her groceries to the porch?" I asked.

"No. The tops of the bags were folded over."

"Ha," I said. Anthony looked away from me.

"Hmm," said Julio.

"Hmm? Oh, right, hmm," I said, suddenly knowing what Julio was thinking.

"What are you talking about?" Rochelle called to us. She had taken about three more steps toward the witch's house. "Can I come back and listen?" As she spoke, she returned to the tree.

"We're not talking. The superstitious peasants are musing," said Julio.

"That means thinking," said Calvin.

"Good man." Julio patted Calvin on the back.

"About what?" asked Anthony.

"About garbage," said Julio.

"Garbage as in thinking about nothing important?" asked The Raven.

"No, garbage as in garbage. Trash. Refuse," said Julio.

"He's gone nuts," said Anthony. "Probably a witch spell."

"I don't think so," I said. "Let's go into the alley behind the witch's house."

"Why?" asked Anthony.

"To look at garbage, of course," I said.

Julio and I were excited as we made our way through the nearest building and into the alley. Everyone else was bugged.

"What garbage do you want to see?" asked Suzie Q.

"Not what, whose," I said.

"Whose, then," she said.

"The witch's garbage," Julio said.

My friends stopped dead in their tracks.

"No way. I'm not going near the witch's garbage," said Suzie Q.

"Me neither," said Calvin.

"I'm not touching anyone's garbage," said Rochelle. "You can get diseases that way."

"We're not asking you to eat it, just look at it," I said.

"I'm going to wup," said Rochelle, turning a greenish color.

"The lady is going to wup," said Julio. "That's the same as throwing up or barfing or tossing one's cookies, Calvin."

"I know some more words for it, too," said Calvin.

"Shut up, guys. If she really gets sick, it will slow us down," I said.

We had reached the alley behind the witch's house. Someone had once built a brick room onto the back of the original wooden farmhouse. It had a steep roof made of thick glass and wire. From the neighboring roofs, it looked like a giant window facing the sky, only you couldn't see through it. Before the Neighborhood Association got started, about one kid a year, usually on a dare, would go to the roof of a nearby building and toss a brick onto the glass. It had never broken. It had never even cracked. In the neighborhood, it came to be known as witch's glass.

There were no garbage cans in the alley behind the brick room. "Of course there wouldn't be cans," said the Raven. "The supers keep the cans in the alleys to keep them from smelling up the inside of the buildings. The witch lives here alone. She probably doesn't make enough garbage to need an alley can."

"Have you ever seen a garbage can or bag in front of her house on garbage days?" I asked.

"No," everyone agreed.

"Maybe you just never noticed," said Rochelle.

"Maybe she doesn't have to eat," said Julio.

"Can we go home now?" asked Calvin.

"Everyone makes garbage," I said, "even if they don't eat. It's a fact of life."

"But is it a fact of witch life?" asked Anthony.

"I think I heard my mother calling me," said Rochelle.

"If you leave now, your name will be dog meat on this block," warned Suzie Q. "If you take off and we find Princess, I'll mail her back to Siam—"

"Thailand," whispered Rochelle.

"—and I'll make you pay for the stamps," Suzie Q finished her threat. Rochelle nodded her head.

"There's a door from the alley into that room," I said.

"So?" everyone asked, scared.

"So, since everyone makes garbage . . . " I began.

" . . . and no one has ever seen her put her garbage out front . . . " said Julio.

" . . . she must come through that door at night and—" I continued.

"—dump her garbage into the cans behind the other buildings," finished Julio.

"The psychic twins are at it again," said Anthony.

I ignored him. "Let's start looking," I said.

"For what?" asked Calvin.

"Dead cats?" whined Rochelle.

"Dead cats?" asked Suzie Q in a shocked voice.

"No, don't be idiots. Empty cat-food cans or boxes or bags. Maybe empty bags of kitty litter. Maybe lots of old chicken bones," I said.

"What if she's feeding the cats hamburger meat?" asked The Raven.

"Don't be a smart-mouth, Raven. Just do whatever Loretta asks so we can get out of here," ordered Suzie Q.

"Sure, baby sister."

We divided up and began searching the garbage cans. It was smelly but important work. Luckily there had been a garbage pick-up the day before, so there wasn't as much mess to go through as there could have been. Also, each garbage bag in the cans had been neatly slit open from top to bottom, so we could see what was in each one without getting our hands dirty.

"BINGO!" shouted Julio. He and Calvin were dancing around a trash can two buildings down from the witch's house. We all rushed over. A paper bag stuffed with empty cat-food cans and an empty ten-pound sack of Crunchy Cruncho's dry cat food were lying on top of the other garbage. Right underneath that evidence were at least a half-dozen empty bags of cat litter.

"We didn't have to dig for it." Julio looked smug and clean.

"Lucky you," grumbled The Raven, wiping his hands on his handkerchief.

"How do we know who the garbage belongs to?" asked Suzie Q. "It could be anybody's."

"No it couldn't," said Julio.

"Why?" asked Calvin.

"Because look at how many empty cans of food are here—and bags of litter. Whoever owns this garbage is taking care of a whole lot of cats. Nobody on our block has that many cats," I said.

"Hardly anybody on the block has a cat at all anymore," said Anthony. "I made a list during lunch. Thirty-three cats are missing from Burnridge Avenue."

"Well, what do we do about it? Should we tell our parents what we found?" asked Rochelle.

"This is our business," said The Raven.

"They wouldn't believe us anyway," said Julio.

"Let's go tell Dad," said Calvin.

"He's working on construction today," I said. "He's too busy. The Raven is right, this is our business."

"Wrong, me darlings." A crackling, high-pitched voice made chills go up our spines. "It's none of your business and it's none of their business—it's *my* business." We turned to see the witch of Burnridge standing behind us. The door into the brick room was standing open.

"We're sunk," moaned The Raven.

"Dead as doorknobs," said Julio.

"Cooked gooses," I said.

"Is she going to make us into gingerbread men?" asked Calvin.

The witch was beckoning to us with a gnarled old finger.

SEVEN

THE WITCH'S PARLOR

I felt my feet moving toward the witch.

"Hold on to me, Suzie Q," I whispered. "I'm walking and I don't want to."

"Me, too," said Suzie Q. Her voice was trembling.

We were bunched together as close as we could get, holding hands. Step by step we walked toward the witch.

"Let go of my chair," said The Raven, "you're dragging me with you."

"Raven," said Julio, "your own hands are pushing the wheels." The Raven looked grim.

"I keep trying to scream for help and I can't," said Suzie Q.

"Me, too. The sounds won't come out of my mouth." I tried yelling for help again. Nothing happened. It was like being in the middle of a nightmare.

Anthony was making strange gagging noises. I turned to look at him. His face was twitching strangely.

"What's happening?" Calvin's voice was shaking.

"I think we're going to visit the witch," I said.

"You bet, dearies," cackled the witch as she stepped aside so we could move through the doorway. "Come into my parlor."

"Where are the Pane Peepers when you need them?" Suzie Q moaned.

"Resting, me nosey one, resting from a morning's hard labor," said the witch, slamming the door behind us. We heard a bolt slide into place.

"I don't want to be here," said Calvin, beginning to cry. We were in the brick room.

"This is certainly not a parlor," said Julio.

"Who cares," I said.

"It's a kitchen," whispered Calvin. "Look at that huge black stove. We're goners for sure."

"It's a garden. Look at the plants." I was impressed. Even in times of peril I love plants.

"It's like a jungle in here." Suzie Q was staring up at an enormous big-leafed philodendron that nearly touched the glass ceiling.

"Sure it is. Witches always live in the woods." Calvin grabbed my hand.

"She said jungle, not woods, brat. Besides, this is neither. We're inside a house. This is just a solarium." Rochelle's voice was nasty.

"Look, Roach, you call my brother a name again and I'll pop you one." I put my arm around Calvin's shoulders.

66

"My name is Rochelle, not Roach."

"That's a matter of opinion." I glared at her.

"What's a solarium?" asked Calvin.

"A room to which the sun has free access—originally—" began Julio.

"Are you all crazy? We've been forced into the witch's house against our wills and you're standing around discussing plants and vocabulary." The Raven sounded disgusted. For about a minute, I didn't care what happened to us. I was in the exact room I had always dreamed of having.

The air in the brick room smelled just like the air in the glass Conservatory at the Botanical Garden—heavy, clean, and rich with growing things. Plants were everywhere. There were huge plants, medium-sized plants, tiny plants—barrels, pots, and boxes of plants—flowering plants, edible plants, herbs, trees, bushes, and vegetables. Enormous feathery ferns hung from a beam, their fronds swaying gently as we moved beneath them. Vines twisted and curled up and down the brick walls.

Light coming through the ceiling made it seem as if we were still outside. But, of course, we weren't. As The Raven had reminded us, we were inside the witch's house.

"Amazing," I whispered.

"Is that where you bake little kids?" asked Calvin.

He was pointing to a corner of the room where an enormous, old-fashioned, cast-iron stove stood alongside a sink and refrigerator. On the wall above were shelves filled with jars and cans and boxes and dishes and pots and pans. In front of the kitchen equipment were a long, wooden table, two benches, and a rocking chair.

"You're sick, Calvin. People don't cook other people." Rochelle looked down her nose at Calvin, who was shaking with fear.

"Witches do," he insisted.

"There are no such things as witches." Rochelle sounded smug.

"Heh. Heh. Heh," said the bent-over witch, hobbling toward us. She reached behind me and gently pinched Rochelle's arm. "Succulent," the witch cackled. "I prefer little girls. Little boys are much too tough."

Rochelle whimpered and Calvin stopped trembling. The witch was holding her shawl tightly around her face. I couldn't see what she looked like. I was sure she was hideous. I could feel her terrible witch-breath move past my ear toward Rochelle.

"You have a remarkable green thumb." I nervously squeaked the words.

"Don't insult her, Loretta." Suzie Q reached over and poked me. "Remember who she is and what she just said about girls."

"That wasn't an insult. It was a compliment," I said, trying not to look the witch in the eye.

"And that's how it was taken, dearie, heh, heh, heh. I'm pleased my little garden meets with your approval."

"Why are you standing around talking about stupid plants when we've been kidnapped?" Rochelle shouted.

"Do you think plants are stupid, little girl?" asked the witch.

"They're just plants. Why are you keeping us here? You're not a witch. You're just a stupid old lady who likes to scare children." Rochelle was on a roll. We backed away from her and huddled together, not wanting to be too close when the witch's wrath fell on Rochelle's head.

"We're gingerbread for sure," Calvin moaned.

"Gingerbread? Are you hungry, little boy?" asked the witch, not taking her eyes off Rochelle.

"I think his question is, are *you*?" said Anthony, giggling. I poked him with my elbow—hard.

"Get a hold of yourself, Anthony," I whispered. Anthony clamped his hand over his mouth, but he didn't seem to be able to stop laughing.

"Fear hysteria," Julio diagnosed. "It'll pass."

"So, are you going to let us go?" demanded Rochelle. "And where is my cat, Champion Princess Ponga, the Jewel of Siam? I'm going straight home and calling the police." Rochelle headed for the door to the alley.

"You are the most unpleasant child I have ever met," the witch croaked as she hobbled toward Rochelle.

The word *help* came out of Rochelle's mouth in a kind of hoarse whisper. The rest of us were frozen in fear. We couldn't have helped Rochelle even if we wanted to, which we didn't. We were sure she had sealed our doom by insulting the witch.

The witch reached toward Rochelle. Rochelle ducked and then slid to the floor in a jellylike heap, covering her head with her arms. The witch leaned across Rochelle and unbolted the door. It swung open.

"Leave," the witch ordered.

Rochelle was whimpering loudly. She did not move.

"Oh, for heaven's sake. Get off the floor and go home." The witch grabbed Rochelle's arm and lifted her to her feet.

"You're very strong for an old lady," said Rochelle.

"A stupid old lady is what you called me a moment ago—or am I actually just a stupid old witch?" The witch growled the words right into Rochelle's face. "Cross me and find out, you small, insignificant, annoying piece of fly food. Heh. Heh. Heh."

"I won't call the police, I promise. I won't even tell my parents—or anyone else. I swear. Just let me go. Please." Rochelle was begging.

"Hey, how about us, Roachy?" asked The Raven.

Rochelle backed out of the open door.

"I'm a master of curses," snarled the witch, "just remember that. Methinks I'll give you a wee sample, dearie." The witch leaped toward Rochelle and grabbed her arm.

"No. *No!* I'm going!" Rochelle struggled to get loose.

The witch's crackly voice filled our hearts with horror. "May your tongue fall out of your mouth, may your hair turn to nasty, squiggly worms, may your feet turn to stone if you breathe a single word of the comings and goings in this place." The witch waved her hand over Rochelle's head, spat on the floor, and then let go of Rochelle's arm. Rochelle tore down the alley at about a hundred miles an hour.

"Do you think she'll tell someone to come rescue us?" asked Calvin.

"Do kangaroos fly?" mumbled Anthony, and doubled over, laughing.

"He's definitely hysterical with fear," said Julio.

"That's what I thought, but now I'm not so sure," I said. "He looks like he's having an awfully good time." Anthony was holding on to the trunk of a small tree to keep himself from falling over.

"If I get out of here alive, Rochelle's a goner," said Suzie Q. "I'm going to get her good."

"A turncoat to the core," said Julio.

"A rat," said The Raven.

"A thoroughly unbearable human being," the witch said as she bolted the door and turned toward us. "I'm sorry, but if I don't lock it, it doesn't stay shut," she apologized in a perfectly normal voice. "Now that that child is gone, let's get down to business. But first, someone mentioned gingerbread a few minutes ago."

"Oh, no," wailed Calvin. "This is it."

"What happened to your witch's voice?" I asked.

"And your witch way of speaking?" asked The Raven.

"Heh, heh, heh," the witch cackled.

"I think maybe it's heh, heh, ha," I said, looking from the witch to Anthony.

"What are you guys talking about? Are you trying to work her up again?" said Suzie Q.

The witch straightened up slowly, stretched her arms over her head and leaned—first to the left, then to the right. She did this a number of times.

"Is that some kind of witch dance?" Suzie Q asked.

"She appears to be exercising," observed Julio.

"Walking hunched over always gives me a backache," said the witch, bending over and touching her toes.

"Then why do you do it?" I asked.

"It's what people seem to expect of the neighborhood witch. Besides, it makes potential miscreants nervous. Would any of you like a snack?" The witch stood up and the shawl fell away from her face.

We couldn't talk for maybe a full minute.

Calvin was the first to speak. "You're not old, and what's a miscreant?"

"You're not ugly," I added.

"And you don't have crooked fingers—or warts." Suzie Q sounded puzzled.

"I hate to say it, but I think Rochelle was right. You're not a witch at all, are you?" said Anthony, who then got so hysterical that he had to sit down on the floor.

"Has Anthony gone nuts?" asked Suzie Q. "Has she witched him?" Anthony fell backwards and rolled around holding his sides.

"I think Anthony, my lifelong friend, has been in on the—

on the—" I looked at Julio for help.

"Hoax," he said. "And a miscreant is an unprincipled person—a bad guy, Calvin."

"Hoax? We've been tricked? How?" asked Suzie Q.

"She's not a witch," I said.

"It depends on what you mean by the word *witch*," said the witch.

"Who are you?" I asked.

"And where is the witch who used to live here?" asked Suzie Q.

"In Florida," said the witch. "Retired. Anyone for milk and cake? I baked a fresh one this morning after I noticed you eyeing this house. I figured you'd show up sometime this weekend."

"How did you see us? Do you have a crystal ball?" Suzie Q asked suspiciously.

"No, I have front windows. I saw you from my parlor. I watched the entire fiasco from my favorite chair."

"What's a parlor?" asked Calvin.

"How come you don't have a crystal ball?" demanded Suzie Q.

"She's not a witch, idiot," said Julio, taking a big risk.

"Yes she is. You heard her curse Rochelle." Suzie Q took a swing at Julio, who ducked.

"It was a ruse—a trick," he explained, "to make Rochelle keep her mouth shut."

"No it wasn't," Suzie Q insisted.

"Yes it was," gasped Anthony from the floor.

"Everyone shut up. Do you hear that?" The Raven ordered.

"What?" asked Calvin.

"Shhhhh," said The Raven.

We were totally quiet. A rhythmic rumbling noise seemed to be coming from everywhere and nowhere.

"OH NO!" shouted The Raven. "The Telltale Heart. She may not be a witch, but she's bricked up the cats of Burnridge behind the wall."

"What are you talking about?" I asked.

"He's being carried away by a work of Edgar Allan Poe," said the witch.

"I am not," insisted The Raven. "If that's not a telltale heart, then what is it?"

"Cats purring. Lots of cats. Too many cats. Hungry cats. Homeless cats. More cats than I ever intended to adopt. Cats in my parlor, cats in my plants, cats in my bedroom, cats in my kitchen . . . " The witch looked desperate.

"Adopt?" I said, amazed.

"Look, why don't we take a snack into my parlor and—"

"Hah! I've heard about what goes on in witches' parlors," said Suzie Q.

"You have?" said the witch.

"What?" I asked. "Tell us."

"Things," said Suzie Q.

The witch took a huge chocolate cake out of the refrigerator and put it on the table. She sliced generous pieces and put them on paper plates. She filled seven glasses with icy-looking milk. She chose a piece of cake for herself, picked up a glass, and headed through a doorway into the house.

"There are forks and napkins in the parlor if you decide to join me. Be careful not to trip on this step—I don't want chocolate and milk all over my clean floor."

"She sounds just like my mother," said The Raven. He looked disappointed as he took a piece of cake.

"Don't eat that. Remember, the witch in 'Snow White' poisoned the apple," warned Calvin.

"And how about Sleeping Beauty," said Suzie Q, grabbing at her brother's snack.

"That was a poisoned spinning wheel," said Julio.

"How do you poison a spinning wheel?" I asked.

"Maybe it was porridge," said Anthony, who had managed to get himself over to the cake.

"Do princesses eat porridge?" I asked, taking a piece of cake for myself.

"NO, LORETTA!" Suzie Q threw herself at me. I dodged just in time to prevent my milk and cake from flying into the air.

"I'm going into her parlor," said The Raven. "It's getting dangerous out here."

"Me, too," said Anthony.

"I'll join you," said Julio, lifting a dish from the table.

"I want a piece of cake, Loretta." Chocolate cake has always been Calvin's favorite food.

"So take one. Are you coming, Suzie Q, or are you going to sit out here and go on a hunger strike?"

"A hunger strike? What for? Are you sure this isn't filled with some strange witch-poison?" Suzie Q was practically drooling as she stared at the remaining piece of cake.

"Pretty sure." I tried to sound casual. Actually, I was still half expecting a witch's spell to turn us into toads or, as Calvin kept insisting, gingerbread men.

Suzie Q, plate and glass in hand, was right behind me as I followed the boys into the witch's parlor.

EIGHT

CATS, CATS EVERYWHERE

I stepped through the doorway and everything went black.

"Turn on the lights, I can't see." I bumped into Calvin. "Sorry, Calvin," I said.

"How did you know it was me?"

"Because you're the shortest person here and I've got my chin on the top of your knobby little head. Suzie Q, please be careful. Walk—"

I was too late with my warning. Suzie Q bashed into me, causing me to stumble into Calvin. "—slowly," I finished, from the middle of a tangle of people.

"I can't see a thing," complained Suzie Q.

"Nobody can, it's dark in here."

"No kidding."

"Get your finger out of my eye."

"Raven, your chair is on my foot."

"Whoever's elbow is in my stomach, move back."

"Which way is back?"

"Maybe it isn't really dark in here. Maybe the witch put a spell on us," said Calvin.

"No, my eyes are starting to adjust a little. I can see shadows," said The Raven, rolling his chair off my foot. "It's just much darker in here than in the other room."

"Sorry," said the witch. "It's the first time I've entertained in my parlor. I closed the curtains this morning so I could watch everything without being seen."

"She calls this 'entertaining,' " I said, rubbing my foot.

"Shh, she's a witch. Don't get her mad," said Suzie Q.

"Are we prisoners or guests?" asked Julio.

A horrible, ear-shattering noise made me grimace.

"Giant rats! Protect your vital parts," The Raven warned.

The room got brighter, and I saw my friends bent over, protecting their stomachs from the giant rats. Metal rings squealed and squeaked against metal rods as the witch pulled back heavy, floor-length curtains from a second window, then a third and fourth. I blinked my eyes a few times and looked around.

"You can straighten up, guys. There are no giant rats in here."

We were standing in a large, bright, cheerful room with wooden floors, white walls lined with waist-high bookshelves, and a big fireplace. There was a sofa, a couple of chairs, some small tables, and a number of round, old-fashioned rugs on the floor. All the soft places—the sofa, the chairs, the rugs, a couple of large cushions—and a few that weren't, were covered with napping, purring cats.

"Cat mystery solved," Anthony announced.

"Grab forks and napkins from the mantle and make yourselves comfortable," said the witch. "Please don't squash any of the cats, and try not to spill any more milk on the floor—it gets the cats worked up."

A number of cats jumped off their perches and ambled over to the milk puddles. A few opened their eyes, yawned, changed positions, and went back to sleep. The rest didn't seem to notice we were there.

"Orange Cat, you're alive!" Calvin flopped down on the floor next to an orange lump. The cat raised her head, sniffed his cake, and took a bite out of the icing.

"She's clean." I was amazed. "Are you sure that's Orange?"

"Are they drugged?" asked Julio as he lifted the limp paw of Tony Tomcat. Tony Tomcat rolled onto his back.

"The witch has been casting spells. The cats are in her power," said Suzie Q, looking around nervously. "We're probably next."

"The cats are in my parlor, not my power, you ninny. I want all of you to sit down this minute," the witch ordered.

"All the seats are taken," I said.

"Move the cats," the witch demanded, "and sit."

"Uh-oh, she's getting angry again," said The Raven. "Lucky for me I'm already sitting. You guys had better do what she says."

A couple of the cats crawled onto laps. Some wandered into the plant room.

"So you're the catnapper of Burnridge," I said. "It explains a whole lot."

"Loretta," Suzie Q warned. "Shhhh."

"And just what do you think it explains, dearie?" asked the witch.

"How cats who had never left home in their lives disappeared."

"Yes, go on," said the witch.

"Go on?" I said.

"You were about to explain how these creatures left their homes." The witch took a big bite of chocolate cake.

"I was?"

The witch nodded.

"I'm not sure." I was embarrassed.

"She witched them here," said Suzie Q.

"I what?"

"You witched them here. You cast a spell and they disappeared from their homes and appeared here."

The witch took a big drink of milk. Her face was doing funny things. She wiped her mouth, got up from her chair, and turned her back to us. She was shaking.

"You did it now. She's angry. We're doomed," said The Raven.

"She'll never let us out of here alive." Suzie Q looked destroyed.

"We're going to be gingerbread people, aren't we, Loretta?" said Calvin.

"Ahhhhhhhh, haaaa, haaaaa." The witch doubled over.

"She's having a witch fit," said Suzie Q.

"She isn't, is she, Anthony?" I said.

"Guess not, Loretta." He had started to laugh again.

"You'll get yours for this, DeRosa," I threatened.

The witch turned around. Tears were running down her cheeks. Her face was bright red. She seemed to be having a difficult time catching her breath.

78

"Why is she crying?" asked Calvin.

"She's not crying," said Julio. "The witch is laughing."

"How do you know? How many witches have you ever seen, neat-freak?" Suzie Q stuffed the remainder of her cake into her mouth and stood up.

The witch put her arms in the air and waved at us.

"She's casting a spell," said Calvin.

The witch shook her head furiously and staggered over to the doorway, blocking it with her body.

"We can run her down," said Suzie Q.

"Try it and her spell will probably turn us into stone," said Calvin.

The witch pointed at Calvin, nodded her head, and began making donkeylike noises.

"See," said Calvin. He scooped up Orange Cat and crawled over to me. "She'll do it."

"The witch won't hurt us because she's not a witch. Tell them, Anthony." I said.

"She's already told them. She's not a witch."

"Then why does she steal cats?" asked Suzie Q.

"She doesn't steal cats, she feeds them," said Anthony.

"What do you mean?" Suzie Q looked confused.

"She feeds—FEEDS—them. She gives them food. They like it. They come back for more. They bring their friends. Their friends bring friends. Being cats, all their friends are cats. They stay for another meal—and another." Anthony stopped to take a bite of cake.

"How do you know all this, Anthony?" asked Julio.

"I know everything about the block," he bragged.

"Yeah, but how *long* have you known all this?" I was angry. "People are really upset about the missing cats. *We're* really upset."

"You knew where the cats were? I'm going to mash you, Anthony." Suzie Q started for Anthony. The Doctor appeared from under the sofa and stood between them.

"Doctor!" A sleek and shiny Doctor ambled over to Suzie Q and rubbed against her legs. She forgot about hurting Anthony.

"Well, Anthony?" I waited for an answer. He mumbled something.

"What did you say?" demanded The Raven.

"I said I didn't know about the cats until yesterday. But I've known Daisy for a while now."

"Who's Daisy?"

"I'm Daisy," said the witch.

"A witch named Daisy?" said The Raven.

"Would you prefer my name to be Esmerelda?" asked the witch.

"It *would* be more suitable for a witch," said Julio.

"But she's not a witch," said Anthony.

"And you, old buddy, never told us, did you?" I said to Anthony. "You let us be scared—"

"Terrified," Julio added.

"And you laughed at us—"

"Reveled in our discomforture," said Julio, "rejoiced in our gullibility and—"

"Shut up, Julio," I said. "I want everyone to understand what went on."

"We understand, I think," said Suzie Q.

"Daisy isn't a witch, right?" asked Calvin.

Right."

"And Anthony played a joke on us and you're mad at him," Calvin finished.

"That's it."

"So how did Daisy get us into her house if she isn't a witch?" asked The Raven.

Anthony looked at Daisy for help.

"Psychology. The power of fear," she said proudly.

"You made us go through that door," The Raven insisted. "I felt it."

"You made yourselves move because you believed I had power over you. It's very tricky and terribly effective, don't you think?"

"Why did you do it?" I asked.

"I wanted to talk to you."

"You could have invited us in," said The Raven.

"Would you have come?" asked Daisy.

"You have a point."

"Do you have anything else for us to eat?" asked Suzie Q.

"Emotional turmoil makes her hungry," explained Julio.

"Everything makes her hungry," said Anthony. "I warned you."

"So you did," said Daisy the witch.

"My stomach is growling," Suzie Q complained.

"How come all I ever do these days is feed mammals? And do you know what cat litter for thirty-two cats costs? And how about veterinarian bills? Every single one of these cats needs to be inoculated—and a bunch of them must be fixed." Daisy ended her speech with a long sigh.

"Thirty-three cats," Julio corrected.

"I know how many I have. The number is thirty-two."

"Are they broken?" asked Calvin.

Julio blushed. "No. When the witch said *fixed*, she meant the cats should be spayed or castrated."

"What's that?" asked Calvin.

"Daisy wants to have the cats operated on so they can't make any more kittens," I explained.

"Will it hurt them?"

"No."

"My stomach is starting to hurt," said Suzie Q. "I'm starving."

"I can't believe it. I just fed you. You're worse than the cats. Well, follow me. I'll see what I have."

"She's not so bad," said Suzie Q.

Daisy walked into the kitchen mumbling.

"What's she saying?" asked The Raven.

"Something about the tail of a newt and blood of a bat. Probably some old family recipe for soup," said Anthony.

Thirty-two cats and six kids followed Daisy into the kitchen. It was a friendly crowd.

NINE

ALL THE WORLD'S A STAGE

Back in the glass-ceilinged room, Daisy pointed to the kitchen corner. "Sit," she ordered.

The Raven placed himself at one end of the long table. The rest of us sat on the benches.

"The witch is trying to trick us," Suzie Q warned.

"She isn't a witch, Suzie Q. You just agreed to that," I said.

"I changed my mind. Everyone knows she's lived in this house forever. Where are her wrinkles? How come she doesn't look old?"

"Because I am *not* old," Daisy insisted.

"Witches always lie to children," said Calvin, "just before they bake them."

"This is getting on my nerves," Daisy complained. "Exactly how long do you think I've lived here?"

"A couple of hundred years," said Suzie Q.

"I'm not even thirty yet," said Daisy.

"Hah!" said Suzie Q. "A witch-lie."

"Maybe she'll make us into cookies," said Calvin.

"Where do you get your information about witches, Calvin?" asked Anthony.

"From a book," said Calvin proudly.

"What book?" asked Julio.

"*Hansel and Gretel*," said Calvin.

"That's a fairy tale, Calvin," Julio explained. "In the end, this person may do dastardly things to us, but most assuredly she will not make us into baked goods."

"STOP!" Daisy's voice boomed at us. Even the cats, who had been milling around begging for food, stopped making noise. "That's better. Now, for the last time, *I am not a witch*. I am an actress."

"An actress?" I said.

"No," said Suzie Q.

"You know, that makes some sense," said The Raven. "An ordinary person couldn't have fooled me. You're talented."

"Thank you."

"Impossible," said Suzie Q, who could never stand being wrong.

"Not impossible," said Julio. "We haven't actually seen her do anything authentically witchy, such as turning us into toads—or cookies." He winked at Calvin, who glared at him.

"She explained how she got us to come into the house," I said. "It wasn't witchcraft, it was psychology."

"Yeah, but what's she doing in this house? And why does she run around dressing weird and talking witch talk and why did she take the cats?" Suzie Q was not giving in.

"ENOUGH!" Daisy hollered. "If you'll all zip your lips for a few minutes, I'll explain." Daisy grabbed the front of her witch dress and pulled. It came apart. Underneath she was wearing jeans and a T-shirt. She flopped into the rocking chair.

"Velcro," she explained. "It's often used on stage costumes."

"What about my snack?" asked Suzie Q.

"Chew on your fingers for a while. I'll feed you when I'm ready."

"She sure is bad tempered," said The Raven.

"It's a new side to my personality," said Daisy.

"How new?" asked Anthony.

"*Brand* new," said Daisy.

"I thought so," said Anthony.

"It's nice to see you two so chummy, but would one of you please tell us what this is all about." I was about to show some bad temper of my own.

"It's my story, so I'll tell it. I'll begin by answering some of *that* child's questions." Daisy pointed to Suzie Q.

"First of all, the house. It belongs to my family, the Smythe-Von Roots. It's been in the family for three hundred years. One of my great-great-great-great-great relatives cleared the land, built the house, and farmed the land."

"How many greats back was he?" asked Calvin.

"I'm not really sure and it was a she not a he—Goody Smythe. Because of her independence and her skill, she got into a fair amount of trouble."

"Was she a witch, too?" Calvin interrupted.

"Not a bad guess, *cupcake*." Daisy licked her lips. Calvin grabbed my arm.

"She's teasing you, Cal." I pried his fingers from my skin where they had made dents.

"Yes and no," said Daisy. "My ancestral grandmother was a skilled herbalist and something of a loner."

"I bet she was accused of being a witch," said Julio.

Daisy smiled at Julio. "I see you've studied American history."

"Goody what's-her-name was in your history book?" said Suzie Q.

"I think the neat young man is referring to the fact that when this country was new, independent women who owned property were targets for those who wanted the property. If the women happened to know about the medicinal value of plants and had the talent to heal sickness, they were accused of being witches." Daisy looked at us to make sure we understood what she was saying.

"I'll explain it to them," said Anthony. "Goody Smythe had property. Goody Smythe was smart. Goody Smythe didn't like to hang around with other people. Goody Smythe didn't have a man to protect her. Goody Smythe was a kind of doctor. The bad people wanted her land. They said she made people well—and made them sick by using spells. They said she was a witch. Get it?"

"What did it matter if they called her a witch?" asked Calvin.

"They weren't very nice to witches in the olden days," I said.

"A slight understatement. If people accused you of being a witch and you couldn't prove otherwise—and you usually couldn't—you were put on trial and then hanged," Julio explained.

"In the Bronx?" I was shocked.

"As far as I know, never in the Bronx, but Goody didn't know that. So she married."

"What difference did that make?" I asked.

"Her husband, Silas Von Root, was an important man. Her property became her husband's," said Daisy. "People lost interest in Goody."

"That wasn't fair," I protested.

"It may not have been fair, but it saved Goody's life—and it began the long line of Smythe-Von Roots who have owned and lived in this house."

"What happened to all the land?" asked Julio.

"Over the centuries it was sold off."

"Have you always lived here?" I asked.

"No. I moved in about five months ago."

"What happened to the other witch—the old one who used to live here?" asked The Raven.

"Aunt Agatha retired to Florida."

"Was she an actress, too?" I asked.

"No, but it was she who came up with the idea of using witch clothing. Smythe-Von Root women have always been smart."

"And crazy," whispered The Raven.

"No, just smart," said Daisy. "When the neighborhood began to get a little rough around the edges, Aunt Agatha used family history to help shape a plan of protection. She knew that people have an unreasonable fear of witches. Aunt Agatha made herself some witch costumes, bought herself a scraggly wig, and began putting them on over her regular clothing when she went to work."

"Regular clothing? Work?"

"Well, how do you think she lived—on air? Phone bills and electric bills have to be paid. She had to buy food and clothing. Aunt Agatha was a legal secretary."

"She showed up to work in a witch outfit?"

"She had an understanding boss. Besides, she'd get to work

early. No client ever saw her in costume."

"What good did it do?" asked The Raven.

"Aunt Agatha traveled safely all over the city—in daylight and darkness—without being bothered once."

"You know, she might have done that without the costume," I suggested.

"Maybe, maybe not. But the kids in the neighborhood also left her alone. In all those years there wasn't one act of vandalism on this property—or a single attempt at robbery—or purse snatching—or anything."

"How come you decided to move here?" asked Suzie Q.

"I didn't decide. When Aunt Agatha announced she was moving to Florida, I was chosen by the family. They took a vote."

"Your mother and father voted to send you to the Bronx?"

"Mother, father, brothers, aunts, uncles, cousins, second cousins, grandparents."

"How many voted?" I asked.

"About four hundred and fifty. We've been here for generations—it's a big group."

"How come *you* won?" said Suzie Q.

"That's rude," I said. "Maybe Daisy is popular."

"I won because, in the entire enormous family of Smythe-Von Roots, I was the only female living in the New York City area. To honor Goody, it's customary to have the Smythe-Von Root homestead cared for by a woman."

"Homestead?"

"That's how the family thinks of it. Not too many Smythe-Von Roots have ever actually seen the house. In the tradition of Goody, Aunt Agatha was something of a hermit. For the past forty years, she discouraged visitors."

"Are these her plants?" I asked.

"They're mine, now. All Smythe-Von Root women have green thumbs."

"And cracked minds," said Suzie Q. "You cackle around the neighborhood like a maniac."

"No, like a witch. It's not easy being a single woman in a city like New York. I'm an actress. I study acting and dancing during the day and earn my living at night—as a waitress in Soho. Do you know how far that is from here? Do you know what it's like being in the subways at two in the morning?

"I dress like a witch and apply witch makeup—you know, warts, a crooked nose, a pointy chin. Late at night I usually jazz up my costume with a glow-in-the-dark skull and a string of fresh garlic, which I hang around my neck—and these." Daisy got up, bent over the sink for a minute or two, and then turned toward us. Her eyes glowed with unearthly light.

"Yeeeeek!" screamed Calvin.

"Yiiiiiiike!" Suzie Q turned pale.

"Don't panic. They're just theatrical contact lenses," said Anthony, as Daisy popped them out of her eyes.

"Those are gruesome," said The Raven.

"Cost me three days' pay but they're worth it. When the light hits them just right, people run away screaming. I'm safe on any bus or subway in the city. The only drawback is I've had some trouble hailing taxis."

"Why do you wear all that stuff when you're walking around the neighborhood?" I asked.

"I don't. I leave off the makeup and contact lenses. All I do is wear the robe and shawl—and cackle and wheeze."

"Why bother?"

"Word gets around. If the kids on the block knew I was a regular single woman, how long do you think I'd be safe traveling around the neighborhood at night?"

"You could learn to fight," suggested Suzie Q.

"Maybe your brain cells do need some nourishment," said the witch, looking at Suzie Q.

"Huh?" said Suzie Q.

"Daisy thinks you need food to help you concentrate," explained Julio. Suzie Q grinned in agreement.

Daisy began pulling some boxes off shelves and taking ice from the refrigerator.

"This table is weird," said Suzie Q, bending over to examine the underside.

"I'm amazed you noticed. It's handmade—no nails in it—wooden pegs hold it together. That table has probably been around this house for two hundred years."

"Don't you want a new one?" said Suzie Q.

"Just eat," said Daisy, as she put a couple of bowls of corn chips and pretzels on the table. "Sorry, I have no soda. Have some iced tea. It's real cheap to make, you know."

"Are you broke?" Calvin asked.

"Who isn't?"

"Then why did you take the cats? We saw all the empty cat-food cans and bags in the garbage. It must cost a fortune."

"Oh yes, the cats." Daisy bit a pretzel in half.

TEN

THE MAGIC OF CATSUP

Daisy lifted the nearest cat into her lap. "While you were picking through the neighborhood garbage, did any of you notice anything unusual?"

"What do you mean?" asked Julio.

"Yes." Anthony and I answered at the same time.

"Does this have anything to do with the cats?" asked Suzie Q.

"It's something more important," said Anthony.

"Is it about Princess Ponga?" Suzie Q sounded excited.

"I've never seen a Siamese cat around here. Don't you think

if I had I would have collected the hundred dollars? Now what did you kids notice?" Daisy spoke to Anthony and me.

"Someone slit all the garbage bags in the cans," I said.

"Who cares? So we have a garbage weirdo in the neighborhood. What about the cats?" Suzie Q pounded on the table.

"Make a dent in that table and I'll put a lifetime curse on you," Daisy warned.

"You're not a witch," said Suzie Q.

"The thing about curses is you don't have to be a witch to use one. Want to try me out?"

"What a grouch," said Suzie Q.

"Maybe you had better tell us about the cats and get it over with," I suggested.

Daisy sighed. "I'll be brief. When I moved in here, I had a bad rodent problem. I needed help. I noticed there were lots of cats in the alley. I thought they were all strays. I cooked up some of Goody Smythe-Von Root's special small-animal recipe and put a couple of bowls of it near my back door. Cats came. They ate. On the third night, the Old One followed me inside—"

"The Old One?" Calvin whispered.

"She must mean The Doctor," I said.

"—and he liked it here. He showed no interest in leaving. I had a cat. I bought a litter box, a scratching post, and a cat bed. He used the box, ate bowls of food, and slept on my bed. He showed no interest in hunting. He was too nice a cat to put back in the street, so I got him his shots and had him fixed. Then I put some more of Goody's recipe in the alley.

"Three cats were waiting for me when I got home from work. They followed me inside. The Old One greeted them like long-lost friends. In the morning, I found four dead rats neatly lined up by the door. Two of the new cats didn't seem to want to go outside, so I bought another litter box, flea collars, and several pounds of ingredients for Goody's stew. The third cat returned in the late afternoon. I hadn't counted on having four cats but they were good company and very useful.

"I left food for my indoor-outdoor cat by the door before leaving each day. That was my mistake. Each night there were more hungry cats wanting to come inside—and each morning fewer of them wanted to leave. It was getting out of hand. Within three weeks, there wasn't rat, mouse, cockroach, or moth in this house. I stopped putting food outside. Unfortunately, by that time, there were cats everywhere.

"I couldn't be ungrateful and evict the animals who had helped me. I couldn't stop feeding them. So I kept buying more supplies and taking as many cats as I could afford to take to the veterinarian. My money and my health were disappearing rapidly. I found myself up at three in the morning cooking Goody's stew because my refrigerator would only hold a two-day supply of the finished product. I need my sleep. An actress with bags under her eyes doesn't get parts—at least not parts she wants. I made a desperate decision. The family had sent me a check to have the plumbing repaired in the homestead. I used part of it to buy ordinary cat food—you found the containers in the garbage.

"An interesting thing happened. I began feeding the felines commercial cat food yesterday. This morning three insisted on going out. Only one has returned. I now believe that many of these cats have been sticking around because of Goody's recipe, not because they needed a home. Goody was a genius.

"That's my story. I didn't know any of the cats were pets— they all ate as if they were starving. No one told me pets were missing until I spoke to Anthony yesterday. I'll be grateful if you'll take the cats with homes to their owners. Any of the strays who want to live here may stay."

"What's in Goody's recipe?" asked Suzie Q.

Daisy glared at her. "A Smythe-Von Root would rather walk on hot coals than give away *that* secret," said Daisy, "but it won't harm anyone if I tell you that a key ingredient is, naturally, catsup."

"Not catnip?" asked Julio.

"Catsup," said Daisy.

"I don't believe it," said The Raven.

"What don't you believe," I asked, "the catsup?"

"No. I don't care if she uses catsup, mustard, or hot sauce in the food. It doesn't make sense that cats who never ever left their fire escapes in their lives ran away from home to eat Goody's stew. How did they know it was here—telepathy?"

"And I don't care if you don't believe it. It's true," insisted Daisy. "What other explanation can there be?"

"I believe her," said Anthony.

"Taking the side of a catnapper?" said Suzie Q menacingly.

"A catnap is a short nap, therefore a catn—" Julio began. We glared at him. He shut up.

"Use your brains, guys," I said. "All of the missing apartment cats live on this side of the street—in nearby buildings— on lower floors—with alley windows and fire escapes. They probably smelled the food from their back windows and couldn't resist it. The rest of the missing pet cats were let out each day."

"Goody's stew does have a powerful odor," said Daisy.

"Then it all fits together," said The Raven. "In a way it's too bad. I liked the thought of having an evil witch who did horrible things for a neighbor." The Raven looked at his watch.

"We'd better get going. It's still early enough to look for Princess."

"Not so fast. We have other business to finish first," said Daisy.

"You mean the vandalized garbage?" said Julio.

"That, and the cats. Would you mind taking some of them with you—the ones who have homes." Daisy sounded desperate.

"Let's go sort them out," I said.

"We won't tell anyone you're not a witch," promised Anthony.

"I have a confession to make. The Neighborhood Watch already knows," said Daisy. "Aunt Agatha introduced me right before she left for Florida. They keep an eye on the homestead when I'm not here."

"They know you're not a witch?" said Suzie Q.

"Of course."

"Sheeesh," said Suzie Q.

"Do they know about you and the cats?" I asked.

Daisy shrugged her shoulders. "They've never said anything."

"We can't take the cats to their homes all at once," announced Julio.

"Why?" asked Anthony.

"Oh, right," I said.

"What's right?" asked The Raven.

"Julio's right," I said.

"About what?" asked Daisy.

"The cats. If we take all of them today, we'll have to tell everyone where we found them. We'll blow your cover."

"We can pretend to find one or two every few days, and in a couple of weeks the problem will be solved and your secret will be safe," The Raven suggested.

"NO!" Daisy shouted. "Sorry. Thanks for your concern, but since so many of my neighbors already know about me, I guess it's time the rest found out. Besides, it's important to get these animals back to their homes—and out of here. Think of my leaking pipes. Take the cats and in no time I'll be able to afford a plumber."

"The kids don't know about you. If word gets out, it will be around the whole neighborhood in an hour—it's too good a story not to tell. You won't be safe at night anymore," I said.

"We can swear everyone to secrecy," Suzie Q suggested.

"We can try," said Julio doubtfully.

"Try. *Try! Please!*" Daisy pleaded. "Take the cats home. Worse comes to worst, I'll start dressing in a gorilla suit."

"You're joking, right?" asked Calvin.

"I'm not sure."

It took four trips for us to deliver more than twenty cats to their happy owners and Orange Cat to Calvin's bedroom. Daisy gave us a small, smelly plastic bag of leftover Goody Smythe-Von Root animal recipe to give each cat owner. She hoped that if the cats ate the stew in their own homes, they'd stick around, hoping they would get more. As it turned out, she didn't have to worry. Most of the cat owners swore they were never letting their cats outside again.

Daisy had put on her witch robe, and we were sitting on her front porch, resting. "That leaves you with only ten cats to take care of," I said.

"If they want to stay, I guess I can live with the idea of ten cats after living with the reality of thirty-two. Are you kids going home now? I'd like to take a nap."

"What about the garbage mystery?" asked Anthony.

"How about looking for Princess Ponga and forgetting about garbage," said Suzie Q.

"Now that we know the wicked witch didn't take her, there's no place left to search. Besides, we have a much more serious problem, don't we, Daisy?" I said.

"I think so."

"What is it?" demanded Suzie Q.

"Someone has been rummaging in the garbage on the block," said Anthony.

"Rummaging?" said Calvin.

"Going through," explained Julio.

"How do you know, and who cares? You sound like Mr. Firestone. Someone has been stealing his garbage. *Really!*"

"You don't get it, do you, Suzie Q?" said The Raven.

"Get what—that we have a garbage thief?"

"Why would someone take garbage?" asked Calvin.

"Garbage has food in it," I said.

"It smells," said Calvin.

"If you're hungry enough, you can't let that stop you," explained Anthony.

"It's a kid. I've seen him late at night when I come home from work. He must live in the neighborhood. I've watched him. He lifts the can covers and carefully sorts through the garbage. He carries a sack, which he fills as he goes along." Daisy sounded very sad.

"Can you imagine being hungry enough to eat out of garbage cans?" The Raven stared into the distance.

"Do you think it's someone we know?" asked Anthony.

"Nobody has much money on the block, but nobody is that poor," I said.

"Are you sure?" asked Daisy.

"Yes," said Anthony, but for once he didn't seem positive.

"Sometimes people keep that kind of thing quiet," said Suzie Q.

"What kind of thing?" asked Calvin.

"Being hungry. Not having enough money for food."

"How do you know that?" I asked.

"Leave her alone," ordered The Raven, and changed the subject. "Why hasn't anyone else seen the boy with the sack?"

"Few people are around at that time of night—*and* he is very cautious. The one time he thought I spotted him, he disappeared like a shadow," said Daisy.

"Maybe he's a werewolf," Suzie Q joked.

"Be serious," said the Raven.

"I am serious," said Suzie Q. "It just—it just—"

"I know," said The Raven, and put his arm around Suzie Q's waist.

"Go home, kids," said Daisy.

"Do you think all he eats is garbage?" Calvin asked Daisy.

"I've been leaving cans of soup and beans in the alley for the past couple of weeks. Now go home." Daisy closed the door.

"She does have a tendency to feed mammals," said Julio.

"She's strange, but I like her," I said. My friends all agreed.

As we left Daisy's front yard, Rochelle came running up to us.

"Did you find Princess Ponga, the Jewel of Siam? Did the witch have her? Did she put a curse on your heads?" Rochelle gibbered at us.

"Get out of my face, Rochelle," I said.

"Suzie Q," Rochelle whined, "here." Rochelle reached into her pocket.

Suzie Q pushed Rochelle aside and silently walked next to The Raven as they headed home. We left Rochelle standing in the street complaining as we returned to our families that evening. Our minds were a million miles from the problem of the missing Siamese cat.

ELEVEN

REAL LIFE

"What's the matter with you guys anyway?" whined Rochelle. "Are you sick or something?"

It was Monday. We were halfway to school and none of my friends had said a word.

"Shut up, rat-mouth rich kid," Suzie Q snarled.

"Rich kid? What's wrong with you, Suzie Q? Have a cup cake." Rochelle nervously dug in her lunch bag.

"It's significant that Rochelle does not take offense at being called rat-mouth," said Julio.

"I'm not hungry, so get out of my face." Suzie Q batted

Rochelle's hand, causing a chocolate cupcake to fly through the air. It landed on the sidewalk.

"Your loss," said Rochelle, looking bugged.

"I've been thinking about how much food we waste," said Calvin, watching the cupcake being mashed underfoot by the crowd of Burnridge kids.

"It's only a cupcake. It's no big deal," said Rochelle.

"You're an idiot," said Suzie Q.

"Can you guess which kid it is?" I whispered to Anthony. I stopped and let the kids from Burnridge pass. I studied their faces, looking for a clue.

My friends stopped with me. "It's no use," said Anthony. "I was up late two nights in a row trying to figure it out. I couldn't."

"Me neither." I said. "Nobody on Burnridge has much money, but nobody is so poor that they have to send their kid to collect food from garbage. I hope." We walked fast to catch up with the Burnridge bunch before they crossed the last street near our school.

"It must be a kid from another block." Julio pushed his way between Anthony and me to add his opinion.

"Shhhhh," I said as we joined the crowd at the corner.

"Why?"

"What's a kid from another block?" We had managed to ditch Rochelle when we stopped. Now she was back, eavesdropping.

"That's why," I said. "This should be our private business."

"Why?" asked Anthony.

"Because Loretta says so," said Suzie Q menacingly.

"Who made Loretta queen?" Rochelle complained. "And what are you all talking about anyway? You're acting weird. Did the witch do something to you?"

"She's not—" began Calvin. I clamped my hand over his mouth.

"She's not what?" asked Rochelle sharply.

"We're here. Have a good day, Cal." I shoved my brother toward his class, which was lining up in the school yard.

"She's not *what?*" Rochelle demanded.

"A horribly bad and destructive witch," said Julio.

"She's not?" Rochelle was definitely suspicious.

"No. As a matter of fact, she's just a run-of-the-mill, ordinary, everyday, nasty, mean, and evil witch," said Anthony. "Nothing special as witches go."

The bell rang and our school day began.

What with being in school and walking home and changing our clothing and ducking Rochelle, it was three-thirty before we were able to talk about the hungry boy again. We were in the alley near Daisy's house, keeping out of Rochelle's sight.

"It *has* to be our secret," I insisted.

"Why?" Calvin asked. "Mom and Dad would help us if they knew."

"He's right, you know," said Julio. "This is one time when adults are more suited to responsible and effective action."

"Bull," said Suzie Q. "Did the adults find the cats?"

"Amazing as it may seem, my little sister has a point," said The Raven. Suzie Q punched him in the arm.

"This is a kid we're talking about, not a cat." Julio looked worried.

"A smart kid who is living somewhere in the neighborhood and who has not been noticed by anyone but Daisy," I said.

"And that was in the middle of the night," added Anthony.

"What I meant was—well, he's a human being. It's too big a responsibility for us," Julio insisted.

101

"Where do you think he lives?" asked Suzie Q, ignoring Julio.

"It could be anywhere—two houses down, right around the corner, or blocks from here."

"Or nowhere," I said.

"Do you think he's a ghost?" said Calvin.

"No. I think he may be homeless," I said.

"But Daisy said he's just a kid." Suzie Q began pacing nervously.

"Lots of kids are homeless."

"Lots of homeless kids are on their own." The Raven studied his hands and adjusted his gloves.

"It's not fair," said Suzie Q.

We leaned against the fence and stared at our feet. I was afraid that if I looked any of my friends in the face, I might begin to cry. Having somebody—a kid like us—living out of garbage cans on our block was almost more than we could bear. We all began to speak at once.

"We have to do something."

"We have to help him."

"First we have to find him."

"Without scaring him away."

"It will mean watching from our windows in the middle of the night."

"Sneaking out, probably."

"Maybe getting into trouble."

"Can't be helped. This is important."

"We need a plan."

"Maybe Daisy can help."

"She's an adult."

"In a way."

"We'll find him."

A simpering voice ended our conversation. "Princess Ponga, the Jewel of Siam, is a *her*, not a him. But I'm glad you've *finally* decided to get serious about looking for her. Where have you been all afternoon? It's been a real pain, finding you."

"Ah, Rochelle, the bottomless vessel of selfish interests, joins our group." Julio smiled at Rochelle.

"Huh?" said Rochelle. "Was that an insult, Julio? And why are you all hanging so close to the witch's house? You checked this place out yesterday, and Princess Ponga, the Jewel of Siam, wasn't here. Right?"

"We have more important things on our minds than Princess Ponga," said Calvin.

"Like what could be more important to all of *you* than my dad's one-hundred-dollar reward?" Rochelle sneered.

"You wouldn't understand," I said, "so just go away."

"You've been witched," said Rochelle.

"You're a dim bulb," said Suzie Q. "Scram, why don't you."

"Let's see if Daisy is home—I'm getting an idea and we'll need her help," I said.

"Who's Daisy?" asked Rochelle.

"The witch." Calvin gave Rochelle his biggest smile as he walked over to Daisy's back door and knocked.

"You're demented, Calvin," said Rochelle. "Stop him, Loretta, he's your little brother."

"Why? Calvin would be much easier to take care of if he were a gingerbread boy—no running around the block, no tricks, no blaming me for things. Go for it, Calvin. Knock louder." I kept a straight face but my friends began to giggle as Calvin pounded on Daisy's door, which suddenly opened, throwing Calvin off balance. He fell forward into Daisy's arms.

Rochelle shrieked. I thought she would faint. "Ah, me pretties, you bring me a tasty snack for my tea," Daisy cackled as she pulled my laughing brother into her house.

"STOP HER! What's the matter with all of you?" Rochelle shouted.

Daisy stuck her head out the door and snarled at Rochelle. "There's only one thing which will stop me from turning this boy—or the rest of you—into delectable goodies." Daisy laughed a terrible laugh.

"And what's that, you wicked witch?" I shouted.

"Other delectable goodies. As you well know, me pretties, my cupboard is bare!"

"She wants food."

"Goodies."

"Snacks."

"Soda."

"Where will we get them?" I lamented. "I'm broke."

"Me, too."

"I'll get them. I will. Who will help me?" Rochelle looked terrified.

"I'll go with you," Anthony volunteered. They left at a run.

"You knocked?" said Daisy in her normal voice.

"We need your help," I said.

"Come in." We stepped around plants and over cats as we made our way to the table. "Sit, but don't expect to get a morsel of food from *me*. I spent my last cash this morning at the veterinarian, getting two more cats neutered."

"Do you hate kittens?" Calvin asked.

"I love kittens, cupcake, but there are too many of them in the world right now. All these cats were once cute kittens and all of them wound up as strays." Daisy sat in the rocker, and The Doctor jumped into her lap.

"Why do you call me cupcake?" asked Calvin.

"Would you prefer gingerbread?" asked Daisy.

Calvin looked embarrassed. "My name is Calvin."

"Okay, cupcake."

"This talk is making me hungry. I hope Rochelle gets here soon with the food," said Suzie Q.

"Weren't all of you a little hard on her?" asked Daisy.

"You helped," said Julio.

"I only played my part—the neighborhood witch."

"Baloney. You set her up—threatening to make Calvin into snack food," said The Raven.

"I was just playing. Who knew she'd believe such nonsense? I was sure you had told her I wasn't a witch."

"Don't blame Daisy. We all did it to Rochelle this time," I said.

"Why?" asked Calvin.

"Because she's such a pain."

"And it's so easy to get her going."

"And she thinks she's better than us."

"But she ran to get food to rescue Calvin," said Suzie Q.

"She did, didn't she."

We sat around petting cats and telling Daisy about our plans to find the hungry boy. Finally, there was a timid knock on the door. Daisy began to walk toward it and changed her mind. "One of you better get the door. If I open it, the kid might pass out."

Anthony staggered into the room carrying two full grocery bags. Rochelle walked slowly but bravely behind him, carrying another heavy bag.

"Is all that food?" asked an amazed Suzie Q.

"Yes," said Rochelle, "and soda. Lots of soda."

"We cleaned out the Firestone junk-food cabinet," said Anthony, putting the bags on the table. "It's health food for us from now on."

"They let you into their house?" I couldn't believe it.

"It was *you* who got banned, not me. Besides, no one was home."

"Well, we can't eat any of that stuff," I said.

"What are you talking about, Loretta?"

"What do you mean?"

"You're crazy."

"Nuts."

"Loretta's right," said Julio. "We got the food under false pretenses."

"What?" said Calvin.

"We used deceit, lies, and falsehoods to obtain the bounty," explained Julio.

"What?" said Suzie Q, reaching for a bag of chips.

"We tricked Rochelle," I said. "She thought she was rescuing Calvin from the witch. She brought all this stuff to trade for his life. We're sorry, Rochelle."

"What?" said Rochelle. "I don't understand any of this. Calvin isn't in danger?"

"And Daisy isn't a witch," said The Raven.

"So you can take the food home," said Suzie Q sadly as she tore open the bag.

"If I leave the food here, will you tell me what's going on?" Rochelle asked.

"We'll tell you even if you take it home with you," said Anthony.

"We will?" said Suzie Q, finishing off the chip in her hand.

"I guess we will," I said.

"As long as it's here, we might as well eat," said Rochelle.

"Oh, good," said Suzie Q, reaching for a can of soda.

106

"You're not half as bad as you seem to be, dearie," said Daisy as she dumped bags of crunchy snacks into bowls.

"You mean it?" asked Rochelle.

"With all me heart," Daisy cackled.

As we stuffed ourselves until we felt a little sick, we swore Rochelle to deadly secrecy and told her everything. In the end, she actually was of some help. Needless to say, I was surprised.

TWELVE

THE BEST-LAID PLANS

"Rochelle had a brilliant idea," said Anthony on the way home.

"She had an idea. I wouldn't say it was brilliant," I mumbled.

"I know you wouldn't." Anthony dug his elbow into my side. I pounded him on the back.

"GIRLS SHOULDN'T ENGAGE IN PHYSICAL VIOLENCE!" shouted Mrs. Gold.

"HE STARTED IT!" I yelled up at her.

"BE A LADY, LORETTA BERNSTEIN, OR I'LL TELL YOUR MOTHER!" added Mrs. Washington, top volume, from her window across the street.

"The Pane Peepers are double-teaming you today." Anthony

smiled his most angelic smile at the old ladies who were at their open windows. They smiled back at him.

"A darling boy," Mrs. Gold called to Mrs. Washington.

"You could probably blow up the block and they'd take your side," I grumbled. "Anyway, they're why Rochelle's idea isn't brilliant."

"Mrs. Gold and Washington?" said Anthony, innocently.

"No, jerk, you know what I mean—the Window Brigade. They're going to spot our signals and sound the alarm."

"In the middle of the night?"

"Some of them stay up late."

"You're just mad that Rochelle had an idea."

"I am not."

"Are too."

"Am not."

We kept that up until we reached my apartment. I slammed the door behind me and listened to Anthony's feet running upstairs.

"Let me in, Loretta."

"Sorry, Calvin." I had forgotten that Calvin was right behind us. I had locked him out.

I dragged Calvin into my room and explained in detail what would happen to him if he dropped even a single hint about our plans to our parents.

"I wouldn't, Loretta, I swear."

"You wouldn't on purpose, but you're excited and something might slip out."

"It won't. My lips are sealed."

"They had better be."

"That's what Suzie Q said to Rochelle."

"I know. Rochelle is a natural blabbermouth."

"But Rochelle tried to save my life."

"You weren't really in danger."

"She didn't know that."

"So she's a brave blabbermouth."

"Dinner! Wash your hands!" My mother called from the kitchen.

"I can't eat anything else, Loretta." Calvin was holding his stomach.

"Force yourself. It's important."

"I can't."

"Then fake it—or else."

Both Calvin and I went to bed early. I set my alarm, wrapped the clock in a sweatshirt, and put it next to my head on the pillow. At ten minutes to midnight, the alarm screamed in my ear. I threw myself on top of it, untangled the sweatshirt, which didn't seem to be muffling the sound, and shut it off. I lay there for a while listening to see if anyone else had heard the noise. When no parent charged into my room, I went to wake Calvin.

Instead of Calvin's face, the flashlight lit up Orange Cat, who was asleep on Calvin's pillow. In a very uncatlike way, she woke up instantly and leaped to her feet. Orange Cat growled, arched her back, and faced me sideways, hissing. The old, scrungy thing was defending the sleeping Calvin, the only living creature she seemed to like.

"Shut up, Orange!" I hissed back at her. She began to moan menacingly. "Calvin, get up, I can't go near your bed," I whispered. Calvin snored peacefully.

"Calvin, this is important. It needs both of us. Get up!" I was desperate. I flashed my light on and off in Calvin's face. He turned away from me. Finally, knowing that time was running out, I grabbed his ankle and yanked him toward me. As his head reached the foot of the bed, his mouth opened to shout. I put my hand over it. He bit me. I did not scream.

"You crud, Calvin. It's me, Loretta. You have to get up. Will you be quiet?" He nodded, and I let go of him.

"Why did you pull me out of bed by my leg?" he complained.

"Because your watch-cat wouldn't let me near your head. Let's go, we're late."

Ours was one of the railroad apartments which had both front and rear windows. Our living room faced the front, and our bedrooms were in the rear. Our parents' room was in the middle of the apartment. Sneaking past their room was key to our plan. If they had left their door open, it would be really tricky. My father was a light sleeper.

"You wait in the living room for my signal," I ordered.

"Why me? What if Dad wakes up? I'll get in trouble."

"Just tell him you got hungry, and on your way to the kitchen you got lost."

"What if the boy shows up in the street?"

"You're really out of it, Calvin. Wake up. We talked about all this before we went to bed. If he shows up in the street, signal Julio like we planned and then signal me."

"Julio first, then you," Calvin yawned.

"*And do not fall asleep!*" I shined the flashlight under my chin and made my meanest face.

"Okay. Okay. See you later."

I went into my room, put on a sweater, grabbed the blanket off my bed, and climbed out onto the fire escape. After a while my eyes adjusted to the darkness of the alley below. The moon was almost full, and its light made strange shadows. Everything looked mysterious. I was on the fire escape only a few minutes when a bright light lit the end of the alley. I leaned against the railing to see what I could and then checked my glow-in-the-dark watch. It was midnight. Daisy's kitchen light had gone on, lighting up her glass roof. She was home from work. For some reason, that made me feel a little braver and more confident. Our plan was taking shape.

Maybe Rochelle's signaling system would work. My plan was for us to watch the street and alleys from our apartments between midnight and two o'clock in the morning to see if we could spot the boy. It was during those hours that Daisy had seen him. We would do this as many nights as was necessary and try to see where he lived. Rochelle thought up the flashlight signal system. She also drew a map of the block and marked where each of us lived and in what direction our windows faced. She said that if we could all immediately know that the boy was around, as many kids as possible could watch where he headed when he left. If one kid lost sight of him, another could watch him.

This would have been a better plan if there were more of us living in more buildings on the block and if all of us had through apartments. For example, Julio's apartment only faced Burnridge. That left the alley on the other side of the street practically unwatched. Rochelle's bedroom faced the alley on the same side of the block as did the Quinn living room. The Raven and Suzie Q would be able to use the windows of their living room only if no other Quinn was staying up late watching television or visiting with friends. If she got home in time, Daisy would watch the corner of 112th Avenue from her parlor.

As for Rochelle, there was no fire escape near her bedroom window. That meant she would have to lean out of her window to watch the alley. Unfortunately, Rochelle was afraid of heights. I knew she would be spending her time holding onto the window frame for dear life and safely leaning out just far enough to watch the Firestone patio directly under her.

The last thing about the plan that made it much less than a sure thing was the fact that there were two brother and sister teams in our spy group, and Anthony lived in the same building as Calvin and me. Much of the block couldn't be seen from the five apartments involved. Julio and I thought we should get a couple of more kids involved.

Rochelle whined that no spy plan was perfect and we should just get on with it. She was backed by The Raven, who thought up the actual signals we were using. One flash meant the boy was in the street. Two flashes, the alley across the street. Three flashes, my alley.

The huge amount of junk food she had eaten that day must have jogged Suzie Q's brain, because she said that since we needed to know which way the boy was heading, the person signaling should move the signal light in the direction the boy walked when he left the block—if he left the block.

So now it was past midnight and I was huddled on my fire escape hugging a borrowed flashlight. If it fell to the ground below, I would owe the Firestones five dollars which I didn't have. When Rochelle handed us the lights, she warned us not to damage them. She also said that if the power went off while her parents were awake, they would notice that the flashlights were missing. If that happened, she was planning to say we made her give them to us. It was amazing how much of a pain Rochelle could be while she was doing something helpful.

I was starting to shiver and was thinking of going inside to get another sweater when Calvin's flashlight started blinking inside the house. I practically threw myself into my room. I raced down the hallway on tiptoe.

"Where is he, Calvin? I didn't understand your signal. Did you flash to Julio?"

"Julio flashed to me," said Calvin.

"How many times?"

"One time, and he pointed his light toward 112th Avenue."

I grabbed the flashlight from Julio and signaled whichever Quinn was watching Burnridge. I couldn't see the boy. I wondered if Anthony was watching the alley or the street. There was much that was wrong with our system.

"There he is," whispered Calvin, "turning the corner onto 112th Avenue."

"Let me see." I pulled Calvin in from the window and leaned out as far as I could. "It couldn't be . . . ," I said.

"Do you recognize him, Loretta?" asked Calvin.

"No, not him."

"Then who?"

"Then nothing. I'm just very tired. I thought I saw something but I couldn't have."

The next morning, my friends and I were at the corner fifteen minutes early.

"Did you see him?" asked Julio.

"Yes," I said. "And I think I saw something else with him."

"Me, too," said Anthony.

"We spotted him in the alley and saw him go into a basement. We figured he might be going through to the street, so we raced to my bedroom to watch for him," said Suzie Q.

"You were both looking out the same window?" I couldn't believe it. "You were supposed to watch out of different windows."

"What does it matter now? It worked, didn't it?" said The Raven. "Besides, I think we saw the same thing you saw, Loretta."

"I was watching the alley," said Rochelle, "but I didn't see anything. What are you all talking about?"

"I don't know how you could have missed him. Yours is the first garbage he probably checks each night," said Julio.

"But my father has been putting chains and a lock on the lid," said Rochelle.

"Right. It's important to protect your garbage from insidious garbage thieves," said Julio.

"Cut it out, guys. Now we know which way he goes when he leaves the block. Tonight we can stake out the corner and follow him." Anthony was excited.

"Not yet," said Julio.

"Right," I agreed. "Not yet."

"Why?" asked Anthony.

"Because we have to be sure he goes to 112th Avenue every night when he leaves—" I began.

"—or we'll find ourselves waiting for nothing at the wrong corner," Julio finished.

"You two mind-reading again? I'm late. See you after school." The Raven took off in the direction of the junior high, and we joined the Burnridge bunch headed for P.S. 46.

"How do you do that?" asked Suzie Q.

"Do what?"

"Finish each other's sentences."

"I've told you a thousand times, we're on the same psychic wavelength," said Julio, and then spent the rest of the walk explaining to Suzie Q what he meant. As usual, it didn't make a whole lot of sense to her or to anyone else who was listening. But such things often don't—at least that's what Julio always says.

A couple of times during the walk Rochelle whined, "But what did you see with the boy?"

We all understood it would not be a good idea to tell her.

THIRTEEN

ON STEALTHY CAT FEET

We spied on the boy every night that week. By Friday afternoon, we were ready to take action.

"We have to do it tonight because if I lose any more sleep,
I'm going to flunk out of school," The Raven complained.

"I almost fell asleep in gym class—on the down part of a
sit-up," said Anthony.

"This is no time for humor," said Julio, yawning.

"I'm not joking."

"You do all realize that we're going to be leaving the block
alone," said Julio, "at night."

"It could mean lifetime grounding," warned Anthony.

"Maybe reform school," said The Raven.

"*You're* allowed off the block," I reminded The Raven.

"*Nobody* is allowed off the block alone at night."

"Reform school?" said Rochelle.

"What? Oh, yeah, they'll send us to prison," said Suzie Q. "Bars, cells, the whole works."

"Or worse," I added.

"Worse? What could be worse?"

"The rack. You know, where they tie you down and stretch you until you're just a little bit taller." The Raven smiled his most grisly smile.

"They're only kidding, Rochelle," said Calvin.

"Why did you tell her?" grumbled Suzie Q.

"Rochelle saved my life."

"No she didn't!" we all shouted.

"Well, I would have if Daisy had been a real witch," insisted Rochelle, putting her arm protectively around Calvin.

"Wear dark colors," I said.

"And everyone bring a flashlight," said Julio.

"What if you lose them?" said Rochelle.

"What do you mean, 'you'?" asked The Raven.

"I can't go sneaking around in the middle of the night without an adult and—"

"Look, Shelly, if you don't want to come along, don't—but your flashlights are coming."

"Forget Shelly. We have plans to go over."

"What time will we meet?"

"Daisy promised to try to come along, right?"

"I'll let her know it's tonight."

"Are we meeting where we said?"

"Let's synchronize our watches."

"Is Daisy coming along?" asked Rochelle.

"If my parents are up, I'm going to have to climb down the fire escape," said Anthony.

"Calvin and I will probably have to join you," I said.

"Daisy is an adult." Rochelle was muttering to herself.

"I'm camping in with The Raven because his room is right next to the apartment door," said Suzie Q.

"I guess I can go along then," said Rochelle to no one in particular.

We had decided to meet at a quarter to midnight on Daisy's porch. We would be hidden by the railing, the tree, and the darkness, and we would have a clear view of the corner. When I went to let Daisy know that we were finally going to act, she wasn't home. I wrote her a note and hoped she got it before she left for work. Friday was her big night for tips at the restaurant, and it was possible that even if Daisy got the note, she might stand us up.

At eleven-thirty, Calvin and I were standing in the dark in my room.

"Did you stuff your bed?" I whispered.

"They won't check," he said.

"Did you anyway?"

"Yes."

"They're up. Company is here."

"I know."

"We'll have to use the fire escape."

"I'm not afraid."

We climbed out my window and silently crept down the metal stairs. We live on the third floor, so we had to make our way past neighbors' windows on two landings. One story above the ground, standing in front of the Wilsons' windows, I realized that we had to lower the movable iron ladder to the ground. Would it squeak horribly and bring all the Wilsons running?

118

Would they call the police when they heard the noise? Worse yet, would they alert the Neighborhood Watch? We could get beaten to a pulp in the dark. I leaned over the railing to judge how far it was to the ground.

"Only a cat could make that jump safely!" a voice hissed in my ear. I whirled around. Anthony was standing behind me.

"I almost screamed, creep." I took a couple of deep breaths.

"Good thing you didn't. What's the trouble?"

"Unlike you, the ladder is going to make a noise when we move it."

"You know that for sure?" he asked.

"No."

"We have to take a chance. It's getting late." Anthony stepped onto the ladder and it slid quietly to the ground. He held on to it while Calvin and I climbed down.

"What if Daisy isn't home?" Calvin whispered.

"We go without her."

"That's illegal," he said. "She's the adult."

We didn't bother explaining to Calvin that we had already done enough wrong to be locked in our rooms until we were eighteen. Why make a little kid nervous? We kept to the shadows and made our way through the alley to Daisy's house. There was no light in the kitchen. We knocked on the back door and waited. The door opened a crack.

"Who is it?" a witchlike voice cackled.

"Who do you think it is?" I said.

"Well, a person can't be too careful, can she," said Daisy, letting us into her dark house.

"Where are the lights?" said Calvin, switching on his flashlight.

"Turn that off!" ordered Daisy.

"Ouch!" I stubbed my toe on a large flowerpot.

"Hold on to me and I'll lead you out of here." Daisy grabbed my hand and I grabbed Anthony and Anthony grabbed Calvin. We only crashed into two pieces of furniture before reaching the front door.

"Why can't we use the flashlights?" asked Calvin, rubbing his shin.

"Because it's important that our eyes adjust to the dark so we can follow the boy. He should be passing by any minute now." Daisy opened the door to the front porch. I could see the shadows of three people. "Who's missing?" I whispered.

"Guess," said Suzie Q.

"She's going to mess everything up," Julio complained.

"She probably won't come at all," I said.

"Shhhhh," Daisy ordered. "The boy's a very cagey kid. If he hears us, he'll disappear."

We settled down and watched as various neighbors came home from Friday-night activities. Lights went on and off in apartments. My watch said we had been there almost fifty minutes. My eyes were closing.

"He's late," whispered Anthony.

"Maybe he's not around tonight."

"Shhhh," said Daisy.

"Look, isn't that him?" The Raven moved casually down the path toward the street. When he was next to the big tree, he ducked behind it and signaled to us. One at a time we ran on tiptoe to join him.

It was the boy. He had a half-full sack slung over his shoulder and was moving quickly toward the corner by sprinting from one shadow to the next. A small, ghostlike blob followed at his heels.

Our plan was simple. All we had to do was follow the boy to wherever he was staying without being mugged or arrested and without being spotted by the Neighborhood Watch, our parents, our neighbors or the mysterious boy, himself.

"Piece of cake," I muttered to myself as Calvin and I ran across the street. "Just what we needed tonight—an almost-full moon."

"How about the streetlights? They never seemed this bright before," said Anthony, ducking into the shadow of a building.

"Keep moving or we'll lose him," said Julio, who was dragging what looked like a tall bundle of dark rags behind him.

"You're wearing your witch's stuff." I hadn't noticed Daisy's clothing in her dark house.

"The color is right and if anyone menaces us, I will menace him back." She reached into her robe and a glowing skull appeared in the middle of the darkness. "There he goes." The skull waved toward the corner.

"That's scary," said Calvin.

"The magic of phosphorescence," said Daisy, as her witch's robes swished toward the next shadow.

We were silent. We were stealthy. We were practically invisible in our dark clothing. We rounded the corner, no more noticeable than a large shadow, and saw the boy turn left.

"How are we going to follow him? That's the Wasteland. There's no place to hide on that block—all the buildings are gone," said The Raven.

"He couldn't live there," said Suzie Q.

"Let's keep moving," I said. "We're too close to home to hang around talking. Someone will see us and turn us in."

We crossed 112th Avenue, slipping along buildings, moving like speedy black blobs through the patches of light. We were just shadows in the Bronx night, closing in on our unsuspecting prey.

FOURTEEN

FOPDOODLES, HODDYPEAKS, AND MOBARDS

"He's gone!" whispered The Raven.

"Impossible," I said.

"Then where is he?"

We had turned onto the Wasteland and flattened ourselves against the side of the corner building—the only one still standing on the block. We leaned forward, stared down the deserted street, and whispered into the darkness.

"Maybe he cut across the rubble."

"Why would he do that?"

"Just look for him, will you?"

"Don't give me orders."

"I didn't give you an order."

"Sshhhh!" I said. "He'll hear us."

"How can he hear us if he isn't there?"

"Yes he is! Yes he is!" Calvin was jumping up and down, pointing and whispering so loud he sounded like a croaking frog.

I clamped my hand over his mouth and looked in the direction of his waving finger. For the second time in a week, Calvin bit me.

"Your brother is dangerous," said Daisy, "but accurate. I see the boy, too. Over there. He appears to be lifting something. Now he seems to have disappeared."

"Into the ground," said Anthony.

"Creepy," said Suzie Q, grabbing my hand.

"Logical," said Julio.

"Is it?" Daisy asked.

"You're right," I said. "It makes sense."

"Does it?"

"Before this, it was pure speculation," said Julio.

"What are you talking about?" demanded Suzie Q.

"The boy's lair," said Julio.

"His hair?"

"His LAIR. His cave. His home," Julio explained.

"They're talking about old basements," said The Raven.

"Ones that survived the demolition," added Anthony.

"Quiet. Listen. Do you hear that?" I whispered.

Running footsteps were moving down 112th Avenue.

"How many are coming?" Suzie Q bent down and picked up a rock.

"It sounds like only one—maybe two," said The Raven.

"What shall we do?"

"Keep in the shadow."

"Grab the creeps."

"Let them pass by."

"Trip them."

"Sshhhhh." We all held our breath as the footsteps reached the corner and stopped. We could hear someone gasping. We hugged the wall with our backs and turned our heads to face the corner. An arm reached around the building. It was followed by a leg and then a face which popped out and back.

"Oh crikey," moaned Suzie Q, letting her rock fall to the ground.

"It couldn't be."

"It is."

"You're kidding."

Once again the face appeared, followed by the skulking, shaking body of Rochelle.

"You're late," The Raven said with a straight face.

"Why didn't you wait for me?"

"We were on Daisy's porch for almost an hour."

"Besides, the point was to follow the boy, not go for an evening stroll with you," I said.

"I can't believe you went onto 112th alone—at night," said Suzie Q.

"I couldn't wake up. Then when I left the house, I locked myself out by mistake." Rochelle's voice was shaking.

"So it was wake up your parents or follow us or stand on Burnridge alone until we got back," said Anthony.

"How did you know where we were?" I asked.

"I was on my stoop when I saw you go around the corner. I ran as fast as I could, but when I got to 112th, you were turning onto the Wasteland."

"But we've been standing here for at least five minutes."

"More."

"Leave her alone. It must have been hard for Rochelle to run down 112th alone. Remember, she's afraid to walk to school with fifty other kids." Calvin defended Rochelle.

"More than fifty."

"Who cares? Are we going to proceed, or shall I go home—thereby depriving you of your adult escort? Such action will instantly turn this escapade into a capital offense by Burnridge law, will it not?" Daisy yawned.

We moved onto the Wasteland. There were no buildings to hide us, no shadows to jump into.

"I think the city puts extra-bright bulbs in these street-lights."

"It's the moon."

"I know the difference between the moon and a streetlight."

"Cut it out. Aren't we here?"

"Where?"

"Where the boy went underground."

"If he went underground."

"He didn't evaporate, did he?"

"Who knows?"

"This is the place."

"How can you be sure?"

"It was near a streetlight."

"Do tell."

"I counted the lights. This is the one."

We turned into the empty lot and began making our way over the building rubble.

"I'll keep watch," said the Raven, eyeing the lot filled with bricks and broken glass and nail-filled boards.

"I bet someone gets a bad cut," whined Rochelle, "which will get infected. Has everyone had tetanus shots? You can get lockjaw and—"

"Shut up and keep looking, Shelly." I was sorry she had found us.

"I don't see any hole in the ground," said Suzie Q.

"What hole?" asked Calvin.

"The entrance to the boy's cave," said Julio.

"It'll be covered," said Daisy. "I saw him moving something just before he disappeared."

"I think I found it!" Julio was yanking at a piece of plywood.

"I'll help," said Suzie Q, giving the wood a two-handed shove. It almost squashed Julio as it fell over.

"Oaf," Julio mumbled.

"What did you say?" demanded Suzie Q.

"Oof," said Julio.

We gathered around the hole in the rubble.

"It looks like an enormous rat hole," said Julio.

"There are handles on what would be the inside of this makeshift door," said Daisy, examining the plywood. "Very ingenious. Whoever lives inside can just pull it shut after him."

"I'm going to go tell Raven," said Suzie Q, leaving abruptly.

"She was afraid we would ask her to go in first."

"No one is going in," I said.

"Why?"

"Because he could take us out one by one as we crawl through the hole."

"Why would he do that?"

"Because we're breaking into his home, probably scaring him half to death."

"NOBODY AND NOTHING SCARES ME!" A voice shouted from the hole. "GO AWAY OR SUFFER THE CON-SEQUENCES!" A terrible metallic din of clanging and banging followed.

"You know what this reminds me of," said Daisy, above the

126

din, "the Wizard of Oz. Someone is trying to trick us into being scared by the noise, which sounds like pots and pans being banged together to me."

The noise stopped. "FOPDOODLES! HODDYPEAKS! MOBARDS!" A different voice screeched from the dark pit.

"The boy has someone with him!" I said.

"Fop whats?" asked Suzie Q, returning to the hole in the rubble.

"DOODLES!" shouted the voice.

"A hoddypeak is like a hoddypoll," said Julio.

"How nice of you to explain," I said.

"GO AWAY OR I'LL GIVE YOU A WHISTERPOOP YOU'LL NEVER FORGET!" The voice sounded old and angry.

"A whisterpoop?" asked Suzie Q.

"The same as a whistersnefet," Julio explained.

"Sometimes you're a pain, Julio." I pointed my flashlight at the hole and, in my most reasonable voice, spoke into the darkness. "Whoever you are, we don't want to hurt you. We just want to help you and the boy. We followed you from Burnridge. We saw him raiding the garbage cans—"

"There's no boy here. You have the wrong house. Go away, you hoddy-noddies." The old voice sounded very sure of itself.

"It's a standoff," said Anthony, yawning.

"Let's rush in, pull them out, and get it over with," said Suzie Q.

"Who's the fopdoodle?" asked the old voice. "Try entering my home uninvited and we will be forced to deal with you most severely—possibly fatally." Whoever it was bashed what sounded like a heavy skillet against something hard.

I tried again. "Look, whoever is in there, we just want to help. We know the boy is there—"

127

Before I could finish, a dark, humanlike shape, moving at about the speed of light, popped out of the hole and landed right in front of my nose. It was swinging something long and dangerous looking. I jumped back.

"What boy?" said the boy menacingly.

"You," I said, taking another two steps backward.

"Grams is right. You're a bunch of hoddypeaks." The boy bashed the end of the pipe he was carrying against the ground.

"Who is Grams?" asked Calvin.

"Get lost, fonkin."

"What did you call him?" growled Suzie Q, putting her face right into the boy's.

"Fonkin, if it's any of your business, gundygut." The boy stood nose to nose with Suzie Q.

"Get me over there!" demanded The Raven. Anthony and Julio rushed to the sidewalk and helped haul The Raven's wheelchair over the rubble. When they reached us, the boy and Suzie Q were still breathing in each other's faces, neither backing down an inch.

"This is stupid!" shouted The Raven, shining his flashlight in their faces. Both bullies were forced to squint, but neither moved.

"Son of a gun," said The Raven.

Daisy, Calvin, Julio, Anthony, and I aimed our lights at the would-be fighters.

"You were wrong," said Calvin.

"A small mistake," said Daisy.

"She's right. It hardly matters," said Julio.

"It matters to me," said The Raven, grinning.

"Drop your weapons, you mobards, or I'll blow you to smithereens!"

"Perhaps I'm just having a bad dream," said Daisy, turning her flashlight toward the voice.

We had been so busy watching Suzie Q and her new enemy that we hadn't seen the other occupant of the basement cave crawl outside.

"This isn't working out the way we planned," I complained.

"Nothing ever does," said Julio.

"Move aside, whiflings, and release my granddaughter!" ordered the old lady who was pointing what looked like a large pistol in our general direction.

"You a girl?" said Suzie Q, into her opponent's face.

"Yeah, what of it. You a girl?" said the girl.

"Yeah, what of it!" said Suzie Q.

"They haven't captured me, Grams," she called over her shoulder.

"Good, then I won't have to shoot anyone." The old lady lowered the gun to her side.

"You got a name?" Suzie Q asked the girl.

"Yeah, do you?"

"Yeah. You first," said Suzie Q.

"No, you."

"Another standoff," said Rochelle.

"Mind your own business, afterling," said the girl.

"Right," said Suzie Q. Then both spoke together.

"Suzie Q." "Windy."

"Wendy?"

"No, Windy. And that's my grandmother, Mrs. Jefferson Davis Hollingswood III."

Hearing her name, the old woman began to speak again. "We've recently moved here from elsewhere. I assume you're our new neighbors come to call. Perhaps you would like tea."

FIFTEEN

FRIENDSHIP ISN'T EASY

"Well, are you going to join us for tea in the sitting room," said Mrs. Jefferson Davis Hollingswood III, waving grandly toward the hole in the ground, "or shall we imbibe on the veranda since the evening is so pleasant?" Then, turning toward the pile of rubble, she called, "Nathan, Nathan, we have guests. Boil the water, slice the cake, unwrap the candied fruit, and take the china tea-service from the cupboard."

"Cake, candied fruit, that sounds good," said Suzie Q.

"Remember, these people shop in garbage cans. Don't eat anything they offer you or you'll get ptomaine poisoning," said Rochelle.

"Shut your mouth," said Windy, stepping up to Rochelle and grabbing her arm.

"What on earth did that little hufty-tufty mean by implying we eat garbage? What manner of people are these new neighbors of ours? I am withdrawing my invitation. Nathan, we shan't be requiring the tea. You may retire for the evening." The old lady held her head high as she walked to the dark hole. Windy gently took her arm and helped ease Mrs. Jefferson Davis Hollingswood III down into her basement home.

"You've got a Nathan living down there, too?" Suzie Q asked.

Windy shook her head. "Nathan was a man who worked for my grandmother's family when she was a girl."

"She's nutty as a fruitcake," said Rochelle.

"One more remark from you and I'll rearrange your face." Windy sounded meaner than Suzie Q at her worst.

"Suzie Q," pleaded Rochelle.

"Don't look at me, Shelly. You shouldn't bad-mouth a person's family." Suzie Q put her hand on The Raven's shoulder.

"Now that we've found you, what are we going to do about you?" asked Daisy.

"DO ABOUT US? HOW ABOUT JUST LEAVING US ALONE!" Windy shouted. And then in a lower voice she said, "Are we bothering anyone? Are you upset about the garbage I take? Do you want me to pay you for it? Would you like us to pay rent to the rats?"

"I'm sorry. I put that badly. We simply want to help." Daisy fiddled with the plastic skull and looked embarrassed.

"Who asked you?"

"Nobody, I guess."

"Aren't you that weird witch person I see wandering around the neighborhood?"

"It's a long story," said Daisy.

"I don't want to hear your story. I just want everyone to leave me and my grandmother alone."

"I want to go home, Loretta." Calvin was leaning most of his weight on me, and my knees were starting to buckle.

"Me, too," said Rochelle. "She's very ungrateful. Besides, I'm beginning to itch. I think these people may have bugs. Many street people do, you know."

I pulled Calvin out of the way as Windy flew at Rochelle. She grabbed Rochelle by the collar and began shaking her. Rochelle looked like a toy that was about to lose its stuffing.

"Puuttt meeee d-d-d-ooo-wn," Rochelle begged. She managed to reach into her pocket and pull out a candy bar. "Hee-rre, haavvve thissss." Rochelle held the candy bar in Windy's face. Windy knocked it to the ground. Suzie Q picked it up and began to unwrap it.

"Rochelle doesn't look too good," said Anthony.

"You going to save her, Suzie Q?" I asked.

Suzie Q took a bite of the candy and shrugged her shoulders. "I don't know. It's late. I'm tired. Besides, I *like* Windy."

In the end, it was Daisy who pried Windy's hands from Rochelle's body.

"Can we visit you tomorrow, in the daylight?" I asked Windy.

"Why?"

I tried to think of something to say which wouldn't make Windy angrier. "We always visit new kids in the neighborhood."

"I bet," said Windy.

"That's not true," said Rochelle.

"Yes it is. I visited *you*, didn't I, pea-brain?"

132

"My mother kicked you out."

"I walked out. She banished me."

"That was on the block, not in the neighborhood," Rochelle insisted. I was about to hit her when Windy interrupted.

"You can come here tomorrow, but leave the mobard home"—Windy jerked her thumb in Rochelle's direction—"and no parents."

"No adults at all," promised Julio.

"We need at least one to get off the block," I said.

"Daisy," said The Raven.

"Who's Daisy?" asked Windy.

"The witch," said Suzie Q.

"Okay. See you tomorrow." Windy righted the piece of plywood and backed into the dark hole, hiding the entrance to her basement from the world.

We were just stepping onto the sidewalk when we heard an unearthly cry: "Meaaaaaa. Meeeeeaaaaaaaaaaa."

I turned around just in time to see a small, light-colored animal squeeze between the plywood and the rubble. It disappeared into the basement.

"Was that a cat, a Siamese cat?" Rochelle was pulling on my sleeve and looking around wildly.

"Was what a cat?"

"That noise."

"What noise?" I asked.

"It was a baby crying," said Suzie Q.

"Or a giant rat making a kill," said The Raven.

"Or a bat. It must have been a bat out here in the middle of nowhere," said Anthony, pretending to look for it.

It wasn't the time or place to tell Rochelle what the rest of us had seen. We snuck back onto Burnridge, Calvin curled up on The Raven's lap, sleeping soundly.

"What are we going to do with her?" asked Julio, pointing to Rochelle.

"Are you sure you're locked out?" I asked. Rochelle nodded.

"I know how she can get in," said Julio.

"You're right!" I said.

Julio and I dragged Rochelle into his building, through the basement, and into the alley. We got her over her patio fence and into Princess Ponga's huge outdoor cage.

"If it doesn't work, we could lock her in and leave her here," I suggested.

"I'm going to get stuck," Rochelle complained as we crawled in after her. We pushed her toward the cat door, which opened into the house. It had been left unlocked in hope that the princess would someday return home on her own.

"You're a skinny kid and that's a medium-sized cat door. If your head and shoulders fit, everything else will. Try."

Rochelle got her head through the cat door, squeezed her shoulders in, and got pinned, arms at her sides.

"You did it wrong, you mobard," said Julio.

We yanked her out and told her to put her arms in first. She got stuck again, but this time she was able to help pull herself through. She complained, we shoved, and finally, with a sort of pop, Rochelle fell into her house.

"I wasn't sure a human being could really get through there," whispered Julio.

"Me either," I giggled.

Rochelle stuck her head back through the door. "What's a mobard?" she asked.

"A clown. A boor. Someone without style or manners." Julio laughed. We climbed out of the cage.

"If you don't let me go with you tomorrow, I'll tell." Rochelle slammed the cat door shut.

"She didn't even bother to say thank you." I bounced a pebble off Rochelle's house.

"You're welcome, huff-nose." Julio spoke to the cat door as he brushed himself off. "Glad we could be of service."

"I think I heard her say 'harumph.' What's a huff-nose?"

"It means the same as hufty-tufty." He laughed and raced me to his building.

"I'll get you tomorrow," I warned, and headed for home. Anthony was waiting for me at the bottom of our stoop with an unconscious Calvin. We dragged him up the stairs, and I managed to get him into bed and cover him without waking my parents or being mauled by Orange Cat. It was three-thirty in the morning when my head touched my pillow. The next thing I knew it was ten-thirty, and my mother was shaking me.

"Loretta, are you sick?" I opened my eyes. They felt as if they had a ton of sand in them. I pulled the pillow over my head.

"I'm fine, Mom. I couldn't sleep very well so I read a book and now I'm tired." In our house, reading late at night on a weekend is permitted.

"Well, it's time to get up. Your brother is having a late breakfast. Get dressed and join him."

After I ate, my mother spoke the dreaded words, "Take your brother outside and mind him."

My parents were headed for Manhattan to shop for some furniture. My mother gave me a five-dollar bill so I could buy lunch for Calvin and me.

"Why can't you shop in the Bronx and take Calvin with you?" I grumbled.

"We wouldn't take Calvin with us no matter where we shopped," said my father.

"I understand completely," I said, wishing I didn't.

"Don't lose that, and bring me change," said my mother as I stuffed the money into my jeans pocket.

"If you're going to work at the construction site today, make sure Calvin doesn't get hurt," said my mother.

"I'm not a baby," said Calvin. "Besides, we're not going there today. Windy—"

I grabbed Calvin and yanked him toward the door. "You almost blew it, jerk," I whispered.

"What were you saying about it being windy?" my mother called after us. "Take a sweater, and if we're late, go to the DeRosas'."

SIXTEEN

IN THE EYE OF
THE BEHOLDER

Calvin and I met Anthony, Julio, Suzie Q, and The Raven in front of Daisy's house.

"Have you been waiting long?" I asked.

"No, we overslept," said The Raven.

"Why are you dressed up, Raven?"

"Who's dressed up?" The Raven was wearing the shirt he usually saved for impressing girls.

Daisy came out of her house wearing jeans, a blue work shirt, and running shoes. She looked about sixteen years old. Rochelle arrived at the same moment.

"Windy told you to stay away," said Anthony.

"So what," said Rochelle.

"So it's *her* house we're visiting. Go home."

"No way. Besides, it's not a *house*, it's a caved-in basement— *and* Windy and her crazy grandmother are squatters. I'm coming along. You can't stop me. Tell them, Loretta." Rochelle smirked at me.

"Last night Shelly said she'd report Windy and her grandmother if we didn't let her come along." I explained.

"Stop calling me Shelly."

"I think I'll mash Shelly into a pulp today," said Suzie Q.

"I think I'll help," I said.

"Cease and desist!" Daisy ordered. "Let the little fink come along." She turned to Rochelle. "If you say one more insulting thing to or about those people, you will get a chance to find out exactly how skilled I am at witchcraft."

Even without the help of makeup or her witch's robes or the garlic and skull, Daisy was able to terrify Rochelle into obedience.

"You're some actress," I said.

"Who's to say I was acting," said Daisy, and gave a horrible witch's cackle.

Daisy waved to the Window Brigade as we crossed the street. Several people waved back. Our trip off the block was legal and official.

As usual, the Wasteland was deserted.

"Maybe they left."

"Maybe they're hiding."

"Maybe they're still sleeping."

"Maybe Windy is going to ambush us."

"Yeah, Mrs. Hollingswood had a pistol last night."

"Make Shelly walk point."

"What's point?" asked Rochelle.

"It means walking in front, looking for enemies."

"I won't do it." Rochelle tried to dig her heels into the concrete sidewalk as Suzie Q pushed her in front of us.

"Look, this is stupid. I'm just going to go over there and knock on the door," I said.

"There is no door," said Rochelle.

"Then I'll knock on whatever's there."

"I'll come with you," said Anthony.

"I want to go, too," said The Raven.

"Let's all go," said Daisy, and we made our way over and through the rubble to the piece of plywood. Before I could pound on it, the wood slid aside and Windy stepped into the sunlight.

She stared at us unsmiling, hands on hips, feet apart. We stared back. Windy was wearing torn cut-off jeans, a worn T-shirt, and old work boots over thin socks. Her hair was ragged and short, like someone had cut it with a dull knife. But despite living underground in the Wasteland and eating food from garbage cans, Windy was clean. Her hair shone, her shorts and shirt were spotless, and her boots looked as if they had been polished.

Finally she spoke. "You brought the whifling."

Julio snorted with laughter. "I don't think she likes you, Shelly."

"We had to bring Rochelle. She said she would tell her parents about you if we didn't," I explained.

"It figures. Where's the weird witch and who's this person?" Windy pointed to Daisy.

"I'm the weird witch. It's my day off." Daisy laughed.

"You look like a kid."

"I'm actually twenty-six. How old are you?"

"Thirteen," said Windy, who seemed to be much older. She

had the saddest eyes I had ever seen. Windy turned to The Raven and said, "Nice shirt."

"I'm The Raven," he said, grinning.

"The graffiti artist? You're good," said Windy.

"You know my work?"

"I get around this neighborhood a whole lot."

"How long have you lived here?" he asked.

"Exactly here? About a month, I think. In the neighborhood—about three months."

"Who's out there, Wendelin? Have our guests arrived? Where on earth has Nathan gotten himself off to? Well, don't shilly-shally around, invite them in," Mrs. Jefferson Davis Hollingswood III called from the basement.

"You might as well come in. That's what you're here for, isn't it—to see the freak show," Windy said angrily as she turned her back on us and climbed into the dark entrance.

I was closest to the entry, so I carefully followed Windy, crawling backwards on my hands and knees into the darkness. I felt around with my foot, trying to avoid falling into a dangerous trap Windy might have set for intruders. I found myself sitting on top of a flight of cement steps. There was enough light for me to see that at the bottom of the stairs was a perfectly normal-looking basement floor.

"You can manage, Raven," I said. "It's a flight of stairs. You come next and let Suzie Q carry your chair."

The Raven was beside me in a flash. We were greeted at the bottom by Windy and her grandmother.

"How do you do. Welcome to our humble home," said Mrs. Hollingswood grandly.

"How do you do," said The Raven, shaking the hand Mrs. Hollingswood had sort of offered to the air between us.

"Where I come from, it is customary for a young man to

stand in the presence of a lady," said Mrs. Hollingswood.

"I would if I could, ma'am," said The Raven as Suzie Q bumped into the basement with his chair. The Raven lifted himself into it.

"I most sincerely beg your pardon, young man, for any offense I may have given," said the old lady.

"No offense taken, ma'am. May I introduce myself. I am called The Raven."

"How very interesting. Are you by any chance a relative of that great American writer Mr. Edgar Allan Poe?"

"A reader, not a relative, ma'am."

"What is all this *ma'am* garbage? Why is he talking like that?" asked Suzie Q.

"He's sweet-talking her," I said.

"He's making an impression," said Anthony, as he tried to see into the basement around us.

"On who?" said Suzie Q.

"Whom," said Julio. "On whom. And the whom in question is the grandmother of the newest lady in The Raven's life."

There were no electric lights in the basement. We stood around letting our eyes adjust. Mrs. Hollingswood put her hand on The Raven's shoulder and together they wandered off into a dim corner. Windy appeared in front of us holding two empty cat-food cans, each with a candle in it.

"We should have brought our flashlights," said Suzie Q.

"My flashlights, remember," said Rochelle, "and give me one of those candles."

"Eat wax," said Windy, and handed one candle to me and one to Suzie Q.

We walked around what had once been a large basement. We could see that someone had worked hard to remove as much of the debris as possible. Every corner that wasn't buried under the partially collapsed ceiling was swept clean. At the back of the basement, as far from the door as possible, someone had neatly spread several layers of newspaper on the floor. On top of the paper rug, two mattresses were made up into beds. At the front of each were several cartons, stacked on their sides so they formed shelves. In the shelves was some folded clothing. Between the beds, someone had put together a table from old boards and bricks. A pile of tattered books, a box of candles, and two framed photographs were on the table.

Windy moved away from us. We followed.

"We have cold water," said Windy. "The pipe coming into this basement wasn't crushed. It's the reason we can stay here. Our last place didn't have water."

Suzie Q held her candle high, and I joined her. There, behind a broken door, in a corner of the half-collapsed basement, was a deep janitor's sink and a toilet. Like the rest of the basement, they were scrubbed as clean as possible. Two folded towels, a bar of soap, a glass with two toothbrushes, and a candle in a cracked cup holder were lined up on a shelf above the sink.

"Do you have a kitchen?" Calvin had a look on his face that a normal kid might have if he were visiting Disneyland.

"Sort of." Windy walked quickly to another part of the room. We stumbled over our own feet and each other trying to keep in the dim circle of candlelight while we followed.

"She can see in the dark," said Suzie Q.

"She just knows the place real well," I said, "so she doesn't need much light to get around."

"I don't need any light at all down here." Windy struck a match and lit another candle, which she placed in the middle of a rickety old kitchen table.

We gasped as the profiles of two faces, bent together in

142

conversation, appeared to float out of the darkness. The Raven and Mrs. Hollingswood were sitting in complete darkness, facing a brick wall. Mrs. Hollingswood was whispering into The Raven's ear and gesturing with her arms. After a few moments, Mrs. Hollingswood turned to us.

"Ah, I see my granddaughter has given you a tour of our country home. Come join us on the screened veranda and enjoy the beauty of my garden. Look at the bougainvillea vines. Aren't they magnificent?" Mrs. Jefferson Davis Hollingswood III smiled at us and turned again to the basement wall.

"They are truly beautiful, ma'am," said The Raven.

"She is truly nuts," said Rochelle.

Windy whirled on Rochelle and grabbed her arm. Daisy stepped between them. "Please let me handle this, Windy." Windy let go of Rochelle.

"I warned you, Miss Mouth." Daisy hissed into Rochelle's ear. "I am now executing the first part of an irreversible curse. I will let you stew in your own juices, wallow in your own muddy fears hoping I do not choose to complete what I have begun." Then Daisy mumbled something to herself. Rochelle looked petrified.

"You're an actress," she whined, "not a witch."

"Am I acting like a witch because I am an actress or pretending to be an actress because I am a witch in hiding? Try making one more unthinking remark and you'll find out, me pretty." Daisy sounded horribly menacing in the basement cave.

"Perhaps Nathan will serve the iced tea now," said Mrs. Hollingswood.

"Nathan is in town at the market, Grams. Why don't I do it?" said Windy.

Windy took Suzie Q's candle from her and moved toward the

last unexplored corner of the basement. There, neatly stacked in a beaten-up old bookcase, were some dishes and cups, a glass, a box of dried cereal, a box of instant milk, a jar of instant tea, two cans of soup, an old camping stove, and two dented pots. Windy put a spoonful of tea in the glass and walked away into the darkness. We could hear her returning before we saw her, the spoon clinking on the glass as she stirred the tea into the water. She handed the glass to Mrs. Hollingswood, who took a sip and turned to The Raven.

"Would you like some sugar in your tea, young sir?"

"No, my tea is just fine," said The Raven, pretending to drink a glass of tea.

"How about a gingersnap? You, young lady, would you mind passing them around since Nathan is presently unavailable." Mrs. Hollingswood handed an imaginary plate to Suzie Q, who took it and offered it around to us.

"This is stu—" began Rochelle.

"Even if the witch doesn't turn you into a bug, I will squash you," warned Suzie Q softly. "Take a gingersnap and eat it. I want to see you chew!"

Rochelle chewed on her imaginary gingersnap. Daisy stepped forward.

"Thank you for having us in your lovely home, Mrs. Hollingswood. I hope you and your granddaughter honor me with a visit to my home which, I am afraid, is not as grand as this."

"We would love to call on you. What is your name, young lady?"

"Daisy."

"Ah, like the pretty flower of the fields. You must all call me Miss Elvina, now that we are acquainted. Wendelin, please show our guests to the door." Mrs. Hollingswood turned back to the wall, took a sip of her tea, and took a deep breath. "The fragrance—ahhhh . . ." we could hear her say to herself as we headed for the basement stairs.

"This is a great place, maybe the best place I've ever been," said Calvin.

Windy looked into Calvin's beaming face and chucked him under the chin. "Thanks, kid. What's your name?"

"Calvin Bernstein."

"A pleasure to know you, Calvin Bernstein."

SEVENTEEN

A FRIEND IN NEED

Windy stood at the entrance to the basement as we made our way to the sidewalk. I turned to take one last look and saw a small, dark-eared cat trot across the lot with a huge dead rat in its mouth. It dropped the awful thing at Windy's feet and rubbed against her leg. I nudged Suzie Q, and she and I crowded Rochelle, pushing her toward the corner. Only Rochelle failed to notice the cat, which, in the daylight, looked exactly like the description we had been given of Champion Princess Ponga, the Jewel of Siam. My friends pushed in around Rochelle and hurried her toward home.

"What's going on here anyway?" she complained.

"It's lunchtime," said Suzie Q.

"Do you think Windy eats three meals a day?" asked Calvin.

"Probably more like one or two, if she's lucky," said Suzie Q.

"I wonder if an occasional bowl of soup and some scraps from the garbage qualify as a meal," said Julio.

"I'm taking her half my lunch today," said Calvin.

"The Raven and I can sneak some food for the two of them," said Suzie Q.

"And just how do you think we're going to get off the block to deliver it?" I asked, looking at Daisy, who was dragging her feet and kicking pebbles as she walked.

"It's okay. I was thinking I'd go back there this afternoon and drop off some cat food before I go to the audition," Daisy said absentmindedly.

"Oh, no," I thought to myself. Anthony groaned; Julio rubbed his rabbit's foot; The Raven crossed his fingers and began to speak rapidly.

"I'm allowed off the block, so I'll take the food to Windy and her grandmother. Maybe we can make some sandwiches—and take some ice so Miss Elvina can have real iced tea and—"

But nothing distracted Rochelle. "CAT FOOD!" she shouted. "Are those people keeping a cat? I heard a cat last night. I heard a *Siamese* cat. You said it was a baby. You said it was a rat. You said it was a bat. It wasn't, was it? You lied to me. Just now I thought I saw a cat running across that dirty lot. Was that my Princess? I'm going back."

We had reached the corner of 112th Avenue and Burnridge. "Alone, Shelly? You're going into a dangerous street like the Wasteland alone? Some drug-head is going to see you sneaking up 112th Avenue, follow you, knock you to the ground, and pull your designer running shoes right off your smelly feet." I was exaggerating a whole lot but I wanted to scare Rochelle. I didn't want her taking Princess away from Windy.

"You're wrong, Loretta," said The Raven. "They're going to wait until Shelly is on her way home, and then they're going to steal her shoes *and* the cat—if, of course, the cat is Princess Ponga, the Jewel of Siam."

"There are a zillion stray cats in the Bronx," said Suzie Q.

"And I bet a large percentage of those are gray," said Julio with a straight face.

"You saw a gray cat? Princess Ponga is tan with dark brown markings." Rochelle was starting to sound uncertain.

"You could be putting your life on the line for a regular old alley cat, Shelly." I stopped in front of the pizza shop.

"Maybe Princess is just dirty from being in the street and she looks grey. I'm going to tell my parents"—Rochelle was getting hysterical again—"and they'll call the police and have those people arrested for stealing. Princess Ponga is very valuable, you know."

"OUTCAST!" shouted Suzie Q, who had been getting angrier and angrier.

"Outcast," I said calmly.

"Outcast," said Julio, Anthony, and The Raven.

"Outcast," added Calvin in a sad little voice.

"You can't make me an outcast," insisted Rochelle.

"Yes we can," I said.

"Only kids who deal drugs are outcasts."

"Wrong. Kids who deliberately go out of their way to seriously hurt other kids on the block are outcasts," said Julio.

"Windy doesn't live on the block." Rochelle was desperately looking around like a cornered chicken.

I decided to rub it on a bit. I folded my arms across my chest and turned my back on her. "*We* say she's a part of this block, Outcast!"

The Raven wheeled his chair around, spat on the ground, and said, "Outcast." Suzie Q silently turned her back on Rochelle, as did Julio and Anthony. Only Calvin faced his former heroine. "Please, Rochelle," he whispered.

Other kids from the block were beginning to get curious and were drifting over. To make a kid an outcast is a deadly serious event on Burnridge. Nobody remembers where the idea came from but it was first tried on Burnridge right after the Neighborhood Watch was formed. It really works but it's so tough that it's only done after most of the kids on the block agree to do it.

Being made an outcast is strictly a kid thing. A kid presents the charges, the accused defends himself if possible, a vote is taken, and, if necessary, the sentence is carried out. Nobody talks to an outcast. Nobody plays with an outcast. Nobody walks to school with an outcast. Nobody looks at an outcast. Nobody hears an outcast, nobody sees an outcast. An outcast doesn't exist—not even to his sisters and brothers. Depending on what a kid has done, being an outcast can last for a day, a week, a month, or forever. Dealing drugs is a forever offense. I figured that turning in a perfectly innocent kid who was just trying to stay alive also rated as a forever offense.

I cleared my throat and said, "Calvin," in a warning voice. He slowly turned his back on Rochelle. A person who stays friends with an outcast becomes an outcast, too.

"What's going on here?"

"Looks like they want to make her an outcast."

"Let's call a block meeting."

"What did the rich kid do?" Kids were arriving on the run now.

"I WON'T TELL! I WON'T TELL!" Rochelle shouted at our backs.

"You swear?" asked Suzie Q over her shoulder.

"I swear."

"On Princess Ponga's life?"

Rochelle only hesitated for a second. "Okay, on her life."

"Kiss your pinkies."

"In front of everyone?"

"Kiss them," Suzie Q ordered as we all turned to watch.

"Outcast alert is off," The Raven announced to the crowd. There were groans of disappointment but questions were avoided by the call to lunch. Everyone took off except Calvin and me.

"What do you want for lunch, Cal?"

"Pizza."

"Good. We'll buy a whole pie and save half for Windy and her grandmother."

"Do you think Miss Elvina eats pizza, Loretta?"

"Probably not, but I bet Windy can convince her it's a cheese sandwich or an omelette or something she's used to."

"Is Miss Elvina crazy, like Rochelle says?"

I thought for a minute. "She's just living in a place inside her head where she's happy, that's all."

"But isn't that crazy?"

"I'm not sure, Calvin. Which is crazier—to live in a basement under an empty lot in the Bronx or to live in a big house with gardens and porches and Nathan who brings you iced tea on hot days?"

"But she's *really* in the basement."

"Is she?"

We walked in to Anagnos Pizza and Greek Specialty Shop. I had to add my entire allowance to my mother's money so I could pay for a whole pie and still have the change she expected. We ate at home and wrapped the leftovers in tin foil.

We hurried over to the Quinn's apartment house, where everyone but Rochelle was waiting. We were all carrying carefully wrapped packages of food.

"Let's get Daisy," I said.

But Daisy wasn't home. There was a plastic bag hanging from her doorknob with a note attached. "Sorry kids, I had to get to an audition—a second callback. Raven, please take this food to Windy and Miss Elvina."

In the bag were a half-dozen cans of cat food and three cans of soup.

"What's a second callback?" asked Suzie Q. Nobody knew but we were glad that Daisy was trying out for a part.

"Well, pile on the packages and I'll be off," said The Raven.

"How are you going to make it over the rubble without us?" asked a worried Suzie Q.

"I'll manage. If I can't do it, I'll just holler for Windy. See you later." The Raven was down the path, across the street, and around the corner before we could say goodbye.

We hung out on Daisy's porch and waited. After a while, Rochelle turned up.

"I didn't tell," she said nervously.

"Keep it that way," I said.

"What are you doing here?" she asked.

"Waiting," said Anthony.

"For what?"

"Just waiting." Some of us were having a hard time being nice to Rochelle.

"Here he comes." Suzie Q sounded relieved.

"Mission accomplished," said The Raven, grinning.

"What took so long?" I asked.

"She didn't want to take the food. Said it was charity."

"What's wrong with charity?" asked Rochelle. "We give my old toys and used clothing to charity every year."

"I think it depends upon who's offering it," Julio began.

The Raven gave Rochelle a deadly look and interrupted Julio. "You ever *get* charity, Shelly? We did, about six years ago when our dad got sick and was out of work. You know what being really broke is? It means every night your baby sister goes to sleep crying because there isn't enough food to fill her stomach. You ever been hungry? Not just lunchtime hungry but hungry so your guts knot up and your head aches and your eyes can't focus."

Rochelle shook her head. She looked frightened. The Raven had backed her against the porch.

"You know what happens after a few days of hardly eating—how about a few weeks, Shelly? You're tired all the time, everything in the world looks hopeless, and you start to give up. Then the rent gets overdue and an eviction notice arrives in the mail and all you can think of is winding up on the street with your furniture and clothing and baby sister and sick father. . . ." The Raven's voice cracked. "Having to take charity stinks."

"We didn't know about your family," I said.

Suzie Q put her arm around her brother's shoulder. "We didn't tell anyone in the neighborhood."

"Why? People would have helped," said Anthony.

"Some things you just don't tell," The Raven said fiercely.

"I guess sometimes it's easier to give help than to take it," I said.

"Most of the time. Maybe it's because there are people like Shelly in the world who blame people for things they have no control over," said Julio.

152

"I do not," said Shelly.

"Yes you do. You learned it from your family. They think poor people are poor on purpose," I said.

"They do not."

"Yes they do. You've told us. You also explained how they think people are homeless because they're careless or lazy or bad in some way." Anthony was showing Rochelle no mercy.

"Well . . . " she began.

"Well nothing." Anthony slammed his hand down on the railing. "How about the kids, the mothers, the old ladies, entire families living on the street? How about the people who lost their jobs and then their apartments and have no savings in the bank? How about people who lost everything they ever owned in a fire? How about Windy and Miss Elvina? What bad things did *they* ever do?"

"Maybe Windy is on drugs—and Miss Elvina *is* nuts," Rochelle offered.

"Sure. In between taking care of an old lady, finding enough food to keep them alive, and making that place into a home, Windy is zonked out of her mind on drugs. Maybe she's a big-time pusher just pretending to be homeless. As for Miss Elvina—when you're right, you're right. Punish the old person because she's confused. Throw her into the street. Make her eat garbage. No, that's too good for her. Let's lock up our garbage. Let's fill in the basement so they have to sleep in the rubble. That'll teach them. And if they survive until Christmas, maybe we'll offer them a turkey dinner. Maybe—"

"Calm down, Anthony." I stepped in front of him. He was about to cry, so I punched him in the arm—hard.

"Hey!" he hollered. I punched him again. "Are you crazy, Loretta?" The tears were gone from his eyes as he grabbed for my hat. I ducked out of his reach.

"You know, real charity isn't a bad thing." We all turned and stared at Julio. "Well, it isn't. After all, we're helping Windy and Miss Elvina and what we're doing is charity—according to *Webster's Dictionary*."

"NO!" The Raven shouted.

"I'm sorry, but it's yes. You think of charity as a handout from a rich person to a poor person—from someone like Rochelle who gives away things she doesn't want or need to people who need them desperately. But a genuine charitable act is one filled with kindness and benevolence and good will and love— like sharing your lunch with someone who is hungry. What I'm saying is that the word *charity* has gotten a bad rap."

"I think I get it," said Calvin, "even if I didn't understand all the words you used."

"Me, too," said The Raven, who had calmed down during Anthony's fit.

"I'm sorry I went off. I just lost it when I thought about my friends being hungry and me not knowing about it." Anthony took a deep breath and sat down on the steps.

"You were just a little kid when it happened." Suzie Q gave Anthony a friendly slap on the head.

"Did you get to eat out of garbage cans?" Rochelle asked.

"Get to? Like it was some kind of after-school activity?" The Raven scowled at Rochelle.

"We started eating once a day in a soup kitchen—then we went on welfare for a while. Any more questions, Shelly?" Suzie Q's blue eyes had gone dark—a sure sign of danger.

It was time to change the subject. "Raven, how did you get Windy to take the food?" I asked.

"By trying to con me. The Raven told me nobody felt sorry for me—they just wanted to share a meal. He also said that Miss Elvina could use some good home cooking—like pizza." Windy stepped out from behind the big tree and sauntered up the path to Daisy's porch.

"In a way you've been eating home cooking from our homes for a while . . . " Rochelle mindlessly blabbed.

Windy didn't even bother looking at Rochelle. She spoke to the rest of us. "Why do you hang around with that lennow-brained wimp?"

"What's *lennow?*" asked Calvin.

"Flabby," said Windy.

"You must have some dictionary at home," said Julio, and then he blushed.

"Don't let it bother you. That *is* my home and I have Mrs. Jefferson Davis Hollingswood III to teach me words. She's better than any dictionary."

"Even when she's on her veranda looking at her garden?" asked Calvin before I could shut him up.

Instead of getting mad at Calvin, Windy smiled at him and answered, "Yes, even when she's on her veranda. Now as for the rest of you—or most of the rest of you—thanks for the food and the ice. That's why I came—to say thank you. If I can ever do you a favor, just let me know." Windy started to leave.

"Wait," I said. "Don't you want to hang out with us for a while? We're kind of waiting for Daisy to get back from Manhattan."

"Miss Elvina is napping now, so I guess it'd be okay. It's nice here. That tree is great." Windy sprawled on the bottom step and stared up at the branches. "Kind of makes you feel you aren't in a city."

We passed the time talking about Daisy and the Bronx. After a while, we got thirsty and a little hungry.

"Let's go sit on Rochelle's stoop," I suggested.

"Why?" asked Windy.

"You'll see." We wandered over to the Firestone stoop. Rochelle went inside, and in moments, the usual assortment of food was shoved out the door.

Windy popped open a can of soda, took a swig, and winked at us. "So the twerp can be useful. Does she always stay inside after provisioning you?"

"No, she doesn't. Rochelle, come out here."

Rochelle slowly opened the door and stepped out onto the stoop. She smiled at us but she was doing her chicken act again—squirming and hopping from foot to foot.

"You said something, didn't you, motor-mouth!" accused Suzie Q.

"I didn't."

"Yes you did. You look guilty. You told your parents about Windy. I'm going to mash you to a pulp and then you're going to be an outcast for the rest of your life!" Suzie Q was red in the face. Windy had gotten to her feet and was holding onto one of Suzie Q's arms.

"I DIDN'T SAY ANYTHING ABOUT WINDY!" Rochelle shouted. "All I said was . . . " Rochelle was suddenly quiet. We all stared at her.

We could hardly hear what she said next. "I told them some of you had spotted Champion Princess Ponga, the Jewel of Siam and knew where she was."

Then Rochelle started wailing. "Look, I miss my cat. I love her. I want her back. I don't think any of you are being fair to me."

"The Firestones are going to call our parents," I said gloomily.

"We can say we never saw the cat. We can back each other up," said Anthony.

"She can't prove anything," said Suzie Q.

"I don't like you anymore, Shelly," said Calvin.

"What if it was Orange Cat?" said Rochelle, meanly.

Calvin thought for a few seconds. "If Orange Cat and Windy loved each other, I'd let Windy keep her."

"Don't sweat it, kids," said Windy, patting Calvin on the shoulder. "The Tipster is a great cat, but if this person really wants her back, she can have her. I'll split the reward with you."

"You knew about the reward?" Rochelle asked.

"The signs were all over the neighborhood. I *can* read."

"Why didn't you bring Princess back and collect it?"

"I like her. Besides, The Tipster's a great ratter."

"Ratter?" choked Rochelle.

"Catches a couple of big ones a day."

"Maybe it's not Princess Ponga after all," said Rochelle.

"Tan cat with dark brown markings on the tips of her ears and tail? She loves to catch those juicy rodents and nibble on their tiny feet and ears. I'm sure it's the same cat."

"Oh, no," moaned Rochelle, and ran into the house holding her mouth.

"Does Prin—excuse me, The Tipster really do that?" I asked.

"No. She likes her food cooked." Windy started laughing.

"So do you make her rattatouille?"

"Or chocolate mouse?"

We couldn't help ourselves—by the time Rochelle came out on the stoop again, we were making one gross cat and rodent joke after another and laughing so hard a couple of us were crying. She slammed down a bunch of soda cans and stomped back into the house.

Windy finally caught her breath. "I have to go now. If Miss

Elvina wakes up and I'm not there, she might wander away."

"Why do you call her Miss Elvina if she's your grandmother?" asked Calvin.

The smile left Windy's face and instead of looking like a regular, happy kid, she looked old again. "It's a long story," was all she'd say.

"I'll walk you home," said The Raven.

"Okay," said Windy.

"We'll go to the corner," said Calvin. We started toward 112th Avenue. Suddenly Windy began running.

"Did we say something we shouldn't have?" said Suzie Q.

"No, look." I pointed to a small figure turning onto the block from 112th Avenue.

"I guess Miss Elvina woke up," said Anthony.

EIGHTEEN

ELDORADO

Windy must have broken a world record running down the block that day. She skidded to a stop in front of Miss Elvina and put her arm around the old lady's shoulders. The rest of us were huffing and puffing when we reached the corner. Windy wasn't even breathing hard. She was talking softly to Miss Elvina, who looked confused and upset.

"It's fine, Grams, I'm here. You found me."

Miss Elvina was wiping tears from her face with a tattered lace handkerchief. "When I awakened, I was alone. It was dark. I called for you and Nathan but there was no answer. I found a candle on a table and managed to light it. That's when I discovered I had been abducted and moved to a basement. I didn't know why. Whoever was holding me hostage hadn't bothered to bind me or lock me in. They underestimated this old woman. I found the stairway and escaped.

"When I got above ground, I couldn't see the house or fields or gardens. I was in an unfamiliar place. I recognized nothing. Then that sweet Tipster appeared. I followed her and here I am. Where are we?"

Sitting beside Miss Elvina, grooming her whiskers and looking extremely smug, was Tipster, also known as Champion Princess Ponga, the Jewel of Siam.

"PRINCESS!" Rochelle shouted, and lunged for the cat.

"Unhand that cat, fiend!" Miss Elvina poked Rochelle with the tip of her cane. "This must be one of the scoundrels who tore me from the comfort of my lovely home." Miss Elvina raised her cane above her head. "I shall throttle you, you white-liver!"

Windy grabbed Miss Elvina's arm midswing. "No, Grams. The cat belongs to her."

"Impossible. Tipster has been in our family for years. Haven't you, old girl." When the old lady said her name, Tipster, aka Champion Princess Ponga, the Jewel of Siam, yowled and leaped out of Rochelle's arms. She strolled up to Miss Elvina and sat down on her foot. "There, that proves it," said Miss Elvina, who was beginning to look as if she needed to sit down, too.

"Why don't you bring your grandmother to Daisy's porch and let her rest for a while," I suggested.

"What about my cat?" Rochelle whined.

"Take it up with the cat, Shelly," said The Raven.

160

We moved slowly across the street. Windy settled Miss Elvina on the rocking chair Daisy kept chained to her porch railing.

"They may be afraid of my spells," Daisy said when we asked her about the chain, "but why tempt fate. I like that chair."

Anthony ran down the block and into Catarina's Candy Store and Soda Fountain. In minutes he was back, carrying a paper bag. "I was going to get a cup of water for Miss Elvina but Catarina said probably hot tea and a muffin would help more." Anthony handed the bag to Windy.

"How much do I owe you?" said Windy, digging into her pocket.

For a second Anthony looked puzzled. "Owe? Nothing. It's a present from Catarina."

"We don't take—" Windy began.

"Charity. We know," said Suzie Q. "But Catarina is always helping people out. She says it makes her feel good. So what's the big deal if Miss Elvina eats a muffin and drinks some tea and it makes both Miss Elvina and Catarina happy?"

"No big deal, I guess," said Windy, unwrapping the muffin for Miss Elvina.

"Where exactly are we, Wendelin?" Miss Elvina whispered to Windy.

"On the porch of the Smythe-Von Root farm, at your nearest neighbor's." Daisy's voice came from behind us. She was leaning out a porch window.

Most of us screamed with surprise. I thought Rochelle was going to faint. "How did you get there?" I gasped.

"I have a key," said Daisy. "It's my house." She was laughing.

"You lied to us. You've been home the whole afternoon,"

Suzie Q accused, trying to cover her embarrassment at being scared.

"Actually, I have been away. I witched myself here from Manhattan a few minutes ago." Daisy pulled her head inside the window and opened the door. "Why don't you all come inside for some refreshments? I bought a bundle of goodies on the way home."

"Can you shop during a witching?" asked Calvin.

"It's a whole lot like time travel—you can get off at different stops to do errands." Daisy winked and giggled.

"You're teasing us," said Calvin. "I bet you took the subway and got here while we were at Rochelle's house."

"If you're a witch, perhaps you can put a spell on the rotters who kidnapped me." Miss Elvina took a sip of her tea.

"I'll do my best, Miss Elvina. Now would you and Windy care to join me?" Daisy helped Miss Elvina out of the rocker and led her into the house. The rest of us followed, including Tipster.

"Princess mustn't sniff noses with other cats," said Rochelle, unsuccessfully trying to grab the cat.

"Why?" I asked, watching Tipster-Princess and about five of Daisy's cats sniffing noses, tails, heads, and feet.

"They'll give her germs."

"Wise up, Shelly. Your little Princess has been living in the Wasteland, killing mice and rats. These other guys have been lounging around Daisy's house doing nothing but eating and sleeping. If anyone's a germ factory, it's Princess, so stop worrying." Suzie Q spoke as she followed Daisy and Miss Elvina.

"You have a lovely parlor," said Miss Elvina.

"I want you to see my garden," said Daisy, steering the old lady through the door to the brick room.

"What's she up to?" I asked no one in particular as I entered the plant room.

"What makes you think she's up to something?" asked The Raven.

"She's giggling and acting mysterious, and look." I pointed to the kitchen table laid out with bottles of soda, a bucket of ice, bowls of potato chips, popcorn, pretzels, and plates of cookies and brownies. It was a feast.

"I bet she even has ice cream for us."

"So what?" said The Raven.

"You know Daisy is too broke to feed the cats and buy all this stuff for no special reason."

Daisy was walking Miss Elvina up and down the crooked rows of plants. Every once in a while they would stop, Miss Elvina would point to a plant with her cane and say something to Daisy. Windy followed a few steps behind them. After the tour was over, Daisy eased Miss Elvina into the kitchen rocking chair.

"Sit, sit, my young friends. We're about to have a celebration!" Daisy pushed and pulled at us until we were all sitting around the table. She filled glasses with ice and soda, took a gallon of ice cream from the freezer, and began dishing it into the bowls.

"I told you so," I said.

"What are we celebrating?" asked Julio.

"In a minute," said Daisy, passing around the drinks.

"Did you win the lottery?" asked Suzie Q, picking up her glass.

"Don't drink yet!" ordered Daisy. Suzie Q slammed her glass onto the table, spilling quite a bit of soda. Daisy hummed to herself as she cleaned up the mess.

"Daisy didn't say anything to Suzie Q about ruining the antique wood," I whispered to The Raven.

"You're too suspicious, Loretta," he whispered back.

Daisy shook a can of whipped cream and swirled an enormous dollop onto each serving of ice cream. She topped that off with bright red cherries.

"Oh, boy," said Calvin.

"I wish I was hungrier," said Anthony. Then, to Daisy he said, "You got it, didn't you?"

Daisy didn't answer him. She stood at the end of the table and held her glass of soda high in the air. "I wish to propose a toast—here's to friendship, our block, the Bronx, the theater, good luck, hard work, talent, cats, and CATS! Drink up, folks." Daisy took a swig of her soda.

"You said cats twice," I said. "What did you mean by it?"

"First drink the toast. It's bad luck if you don't."

We all took a drink.

"This iced tea has bubbles in it," said Miss Elvina.

"It's soda, Grams," Windy explained.

"Do tell." The old lady delicately took a spoonful of ice cream. "This is very fine strawberry frozen cream. I would like your recipe if you wouldn't mind sharing it."

"Daisy didn't make the ice cream, she bought it," Windy explained.

"What a good idea. Very practical." Miss Elvina helped herself to a brownie.

"Are you going to explain yourself or not?" I asked.

"I GOT A PART IN A PLAY!" Daisy shouted. "Well, actually, I'm an understudy. But I am an employed actress! Rehearsals begin next week and we go on the road in a month."

"Congratulations!"

"That's great!"

"Super!"

"Wait a minute, what's going on the road?"

"I've gotten a job with a traveling company—a road company. We're booked into theaters all over the country."

"Then you won't be coming home at night," said Anthony.

"Of course not," said Daisy, swatting a cat away from her ice cream.

"What about your cats?" asked Julio.

"And your plants?" I looked around at the hundreds of plants, which would die without water and care.

"Why did you say cats twice?" asked Calvin.

"Because that's the name of the play I'm in. *Cats*. Having all these cats really helped me with my dancing and acting. Isn't it marvelous?"

"You never told us you could dance," said Julio.

"I dance, I sing, I act, I HAVE AN ACTING JOB!" Daisy leaped out of her chair and did a catlike dance around a couple of plants.

"You're not answering the important questions," I complained. "How long will you be gone and what happens to the cats and plants when you're not here?" I was getting pretty annoyed.

"Yeah, are you going to throw them onto the street now that you don't need them anymore?" said Suzie Q.

"I would *never* do that. I *love* these cats. I thought I might give you kids a key and have you take care of things until I get back." Daisy gave us a radiant smile.

"And how long will you be gone? A week! A month! Two months? I knew this party wasn't free," I grumbled.

"About six or eight months." Daisy mumbled so we could

hardly hear her. She was trying to look cute and innocent.

"SIX OR EIGHT MONTHS!" I hollered. "That's an awfully big favor you're asking us."

"How much will you pay?" said Suzie Q, calmly.

"What?" Daisy looked totally surprised.

"How much will you pay us to take care of things?"

"Pay?" said Daisy.

"Yeah, money. Cash. Dollars and cents. You'll be working."

"I'll send you money for cat food and litter," said Daisy. "I won't be earning a large salary and—"

"I adore cats—and plants." The Doctor had made himself comfortable in Miss Elvina's lap, where he was licking whipped cream from her spoon. "If I didn't have my own lovely home to care for, Wendelin and I could look after things while you were gone." Then Miss Elvina laughed and said, "You think I'm a balmy old fool, don't you? Well, my dears, sometimes the view out the windows of the past is much clearer and more pleasant than any view of the present. Pity."

We looked at each other and then at Daisy. Daisy seemed thoughtful, but she wasn't speaking. Windy sat very still and stared at the table.

It was The Raven who broke the silence. He spoke in a soft but powerful voice.

> Gaily bedight,
> A Gallant Knight,
> In sunshine and in shadow,
> Had journeyed long,
> Singing a song,
> In search of Eldorado.
>
> But he grew old—
> This knight so bold—

And o'er his heart a shadow
    Fell as he found
    No spot of ground
That looked like Eldorado.

    And, as his strength
    Failed him at length,
He met a pilgrim shadow—
    "Shadow," said he,
    "Where can it be—
This land of Eldorado?"

Miss Elvina got a faraway look in her eyes. A single tear ran down her cheek, and when she interrupted The Raven to finish the poem, her voice was sad but steady.

    "Over the Mountains
    Of the Moon,
Down the Valley of the Shadow,
    Ride, boldly ride,"
    The shade replied—
"If you seek for Eldorado."

"Edgar Allan Poe knew," she said softly, and pushed The Doctor onto the floor. Miss Elvina struggled out of the chair, stood up straight, and reached for Daisy's hand.

"Thank you, Miss Daisy, for your gracious hospitality. The hour is growing late and my young friend and I must return to our home before the streets become unsafe. As you know, we do not exactly live in a populated place."

Then she turned to Rochelle. "You are, without a doubt, one of the more unpleasant children I have met in my long life.

Fortunately, nothing is irreversible. You can change if you wish. I shall leave Tipster with you. Perhaps she will be able to guide you in your search."

"What search?" asked Rochelle.

"The search for a better personality, of course," said Miss Elvina.

"Grams, that wasn't nice," said Windy.

"You may resume calling me Miss Elvina, and I shall once more call you by your rightful name, Windy. The time for pretense has ended. As for being nice, sometimes being nice isn't being kind. Let your mind dwell on that as we stroll home. Good-bye, children, most of you are a credit to the Bronx."

We followed Miss Elvina and Windy into the parlor. As Windy opened the front door, Miss Elvina again turned to Rochelle. "Make sure Tipster gets plenty of calcium and good protein during the next seven weeks. It will assure a healthy delivery for her and her kittens."

"What kittens?" demanded Rochelle.

"Really, my dear, if you and your family didn't want kittens, you should have had the cat spayed or kept her confined to your home." Miss Elvina left the house.

"Champion King Royal of Siam was supposed to be her mate," moaned Rochelle.

"Tipster has apparently made another choice," said Miss Elvina over her shoulder. "Despite some bad moments, this has been an altogether fine day, hasn't it, Windy?" Miss Elvina slipped her hand through Windy's arm.

"Yes, ma'am," said Windy, who waved to us as they stepped off the path onto Burnridge.

"I don't understand," said Calvin.

"What don't you understand?" I asked.

"Everything. Why The Raven said a poem. What's Eldorado? Who they are? Where Daisy is going? What's going to happen to the cats? If Miss Elvina knows where she's living. Everything."

"Me neither," said Suzie Q.

"I understand some of it," I said.

"Me, too," said Julio.

"I think I do, too," said Anthony.

"You're going to be a mommy, Princess," Rochelle cooed into her cat's ear.

"In Spanish, *el dorado* means the golden place or region," said Julio.

"Some say Eldorado is a city of gold," said The Raven.

"Is it a real city?" asked Calvin.

"Or a real place?" asked Suzie Q.

"I guess it's as real as Miss Elvina's veranda and garden," said The Raven.

"So Eldorado is a dream," said Calvin.

"Or the thing you most want in the world," I added.

"And can't get," finished Julio.

"But in the poem, the shadow tells the old knight he can find Eldorado if he keeps looking," insisted Calvin.

"Down the Valley of the Shadow," said Daisy. "That's the Valley of the Shadow of Death."

"You mean the old knight will only find his dream when he dies? That stinks," said Suzie Q.

"Heaven stinks?" asked Rochelle. "I'm going to tell your mother you said that."

"Tell her what you want, whiffleball," said Suzie Q, glaring at Rochelle.

"I think you mean whifling," Julio corrected.

"Whatever. What stinks is that Miss Elvina has to live in a basement under a bunch of garbage for the rest of her life and not in a garden."

"I guess lots of people don't get their wishes," I said, taking off my forest-ranger hat and dusting the brim.

"Well, it stinks anyway," said Suzie Q.

"She's right," said The Raven.

"I want to go home, Loretta." Calvin was holding back tears.

"NOBODY IS GOING HOME!" The Raven shouted.

"What do you mean?" I asked.

"We're staying here and having a meeting. We'll call our parents from Daisy's phone and tell them she invited us to dinner."

"We will?"

"You will?"

"But it's six o'clock. They probably have dinner waiting for us. They're going to say no," said Anthony.

"They'll agree. Tell them you'll eat leftovers tomorrow and not complain. Tell them Daisy is having a celebration party because she got an acting job today." The Raven was shooing us past Daisy and into the house.

"What will I feed all of you?" she moaned.

"Who's hungry after all the junk we stuffed into our faces today?" I said.

"I'm going to want dinner later," said Suzie Q.

"Me, too," said Calvin.

"I guess I will, too," said Anthony.

"Forget your stomachs. We have phone calls to make," said The Raven.

We lined up at the phone, silently practicing what we were about to tell our parents.

NINETEEN

KEEPING THE CAT IN THE BAG

My friends made me call home first. When I hung up, I handed the phone to Julio.

"Tell us, Loretta—did your honorable mother, Mrs. Bernstein, the skeptic of the Bronx, believe that Daisy had invited us to a celebration dinner?"

"Did Julio call Mom a bad name?" Calvin balled his right hand into a fist.

"No, I didn't. A skeptic is a person who doubts the truth of any statement, belief, or theory," said Julio.

"Huh?" said Calvin.

"It's someone who doesn't believe everything she's told," I said. "It happens to be an excellent way to be."

"You ought to know, Loretta—you're getting more like your mom every day," said The Raven.

"Thank you. If you must know, my mother said that the story of Daisy inviting us to a celebration dinner sounded as phony as a three-dollar bill. She said she knows we are up to something, which is fine with her, but if we go off the block or get into trouble, we're mashed potatoes—all of us."

"Mashed potatoes—is that bad?" Julio laughed.

"My mother hates mashed potatoes."

"Mine hates rutabaga," said Suzie Q.

"We are *not* talking about vegetables. We're talking about getting permission to stay here."

"It's for dinner, isn't it?" Suzie Q insisted.

"It's for a meeting!" I shouted. Sometimes Suzie Q makes me nuts.

"Will you all be quiet so I can make my call. When I tell my mother that Mrs. Bernstein is letting Loretta and Calvin stay—leaving out the mashed potatoes, of course—my mother will definitely say yes, too." Julio dialed his home number.

In about fifteen minutes, all the phone calls had been made. Everyone but Rochelle had permission to stay at Daisy's house. Rochelle made the mistake of telling her parents we had found Champion Princess Ponga, the Jewel of Siam. They wanted the cat home.

"They said I could come back here in a while. They said it is extremely nice, having a member of the artistic community of New York on the block who is willing to entertain children." Rochelle picked up Tipster-Princess.

"Entertain? We're talking about a dinner that will probably consist of cat kibble," said Julio.

172

Before anyone else could comment, Rochelle was gone.

"That's it, then," said The Raven. "We can get started."

"With what?" I asked.

"With the business at hand."

"Nobody knows what you're talking about, Raven," complained Suzie Q.

"Why here? Who invited you? What am I going to feed all of you?" Daisy marched into the kitchen, leading a parade of cats. We followed.

"Nobody is hungry yet. Besides, isn't that spaghetti on the shelf?" I asked, pointing to a shelf crammed with boxes.

"And soup?" Anthony pointed to a long shelf stacked three deep and two high with every flavor of canned and dried soup imaginable.

"Of course. No actress in her right mind would be without a year's supply of spaghetti and soup to get her through the slow times."

"We'll cook some of your stockpile," I said.

"I'm thrilled," Daisy muttered.

"I'll make the sauce," said Anthony, pulling over a stepladder so he could examine Daisy's shelves at close range.

"Does he know what he's doing?" asked Daisy as Anthony removed cans and jars and bottles from the shelves. He dove into the refrigerator and came out with two handfuls of vegetables.

"Who knows. His uncle is a chef in an expensive restaurant. Maybe he taught Anthony something. Anyway, who cares? Nobody's going to eat. I want to know why we are all here. How about telling us, Raven," I said.

The Raven said one word. "Eldorado." He leaned back and smiled at us mysteriously.

"That poem again," groaned Suzie Q. "It's depressing."

"Maybe he means the golden city," said Julio.

"Or the mysterious region of gold," said Anthony, as he chopped onions and green peppers.

"Are you playing games with us, Raven?" I asked.

"Windy's scrambled his brains," said Anthony, moving away from the sink. He put a large pot on the stove and poured in some olive oil.

"Get on with it, Raven. This is my house and you have invited your friends to use my telephone, my kitchen, and my food. I think I deserve an explanation—one to the point." Daisy plunked herself down on a corner of a bench nearest The Raven and leaned toward him. "I am in your face, dearie. Talk!" she demanded in her best witch voice.

The Raven ignored her. "It's just so nice having an idea without those two"—The Raven pointed to Julio and me— "taking it over, changing it and—"

"Improving it," Julio interrupted.

"—butting in," The Raven corrected him. "At any rate, I have this idea that's so good, so perfect . . ."

"If you have an idea—and I am beginning to doubt it," said Daisy, "you had better spit it out—immediately."

"You all like garlic, don't you?" asked Anthony, dropping a handful into the pot.

"There are more important things going on here than making spaghetti sauce," complained The Raven.

"I haven't heard any of them yet," said Anthony, throwing the chopped vegetables on top of the garlic.

"Eldorado," said The Raven. "Get it?"

"NO!" We shouted.

"Either say what you mean or everyone go home!" ordered Daisy.

"Boy, are you touchy all of a sudden," said The Raven.

"Look, everyone has his own Eldorado—his own dream. Daisy wants to be an actress. Loretta wants to be a forest ranger. I think I'd like to be a great painter some day."

"I'm starting to understand," said Julio. "The last thing in the world I'd want in life is to live in a forest—"

"—and I could never spend my life playing make-believe on the stage," I said.

"I *act*, I do not play make-believe," said Daisy.

"The point is—" The Raven began.

"—that *your* Eldorado is going to be different from *my* Eldorado—" Julio chimed in.

"—and the goal that is wonderful for one person might be terrible—" I added.

"—or boring or not right or ordinary for someone else," The Raven finished.

"These are very deep thoughts," said Daisy, "but what do they have to do with you making a serious dent in my emergency food supplies?"

"I think I understand," said Anthony, pouring several cans of tomato sauce into the pot.

"I think all of you just didn't want to go home yet." Daisy got up, took a bowl out of the refrigerator, and spooned Goody's recipe into a bunch of dishes. "Come and get it!" she called. Cats strolled, ran, leaped, and tumbled toward their dinner.

Anthony turned down the flame on the stove and put a lid on the pot. "This is all about Windy and Miss Elvina, isn't it, Raven."

"What about them?" asked Daisy nervously.

"I know. I know," said Calvin. "Miss Elvina wants to be in a garden more than anything else in the world, and you have a garden here." Calvin waved his arm toward the hundreds of plants.

175

"Is that what you're leading up to, Raven?" asked Daisy.

The Raven smiled sweetly at Daisy.

"It's impossible. Out of the question. I'm going away. This is my family's homestead. I can't let total strangers live here. And if I did, how would I get them to leave when I return? No. Absolutely no. Is the spaghetti sauce ready yet, Anthony? You can eat your dinner and go home." Daisy's voice cracked on the last sentence.

"How can you think about spaghetti at a time like this?" asked Suzie Q.

Daisy rolled her eyes toward the ceiling and sighed. "You know they're not even related to each other."

"Miss Elvina is Windy's grandmother," said The Raven.

"I don't think so," I said.

"Whose side are you on, Loretta?" The Raven snapped at me.

"Theirs, but the truth is the truth. Miss Elvina told Windy to stop calling her Grams. You heard her."

"Maybe that's just their way. They're not from the Bronx," said The Raven.

We were interrupted by a knock on the front door. Daisy left and returned with Rochelle, who looked very pleased with herself. She walked over to us, reached into her pocket, pulled out a wad of money, and spread it on the table.

"The hundred-dollar reward for Princess Ponga of Siam. It's yours," she announced.

"Wow."

"Unbelievable."

"What did you tell your parents, Rochelle?" I asked. "Did you mention Windy or Miss Elvina?"

"I would never let the cat out of the bag. I told them you found Princess wandering in the alley."

176

"Who has a cat in a bag?" asked Calvin.

"It's an expression. It means I would never tell the secret," said Rochelle.

"The money doesn't belong to us," I said. "It belongs to Windy and Miss Elvina. They took care of Princess and they gave her back to Rochelle."

"They can use it to rent an apartment," said Calvin, happily.

"It's not nearly enough," said Anthony, "even on the worst block in the neighborhood."

"Living is expensive," said Julio to no one in particular.

Daisy began to fill a huge pot with water. "I'll cook the spaghetti so we can eat. We can celebrate my new job and the reward at the same time."

"Celebrate? You're kidding. I'm not hungry. I'm going home." Suzie Q stood up. "Are you coming, Raven?"

"I'm not hungry, either," I said. "I'll go with you."

"Me, too."

"Me, too."

We got up and headed for the door.

TWENTY

THE IMPOSSIBLE DREAM

"OKAY, LEAVE! WHAT DO I CARE?" Daisy shouted. "Besides, you've got that poem all wrong. Eldorado isn't just a dream. Don't you understand? It's an *impossible* dream."

"It is *not!*" The Raven whirled around and faced Daisy.

"Is *too!* I studied it in Literature 101 in college."

"BULL!" The Raven shouted.

"What's going on here?" asked Rochelle. "What's wrong? Why are you all leaving? Did I do something?"

"Not this time," said Suzie Q. "Got any candy bars on you?"

"I thought you said you weren't hungry." Rochelle dug into her pocket.

"They're all sulking," said Daisy.

"We are not sulking. We're protesting," I said.

"I thought you were a nice person," said Calvin to Daisy.

"Only when it's no trouble for her." The Raven's face was twisted in anger.

"You kids have no understanding of real life. Some things just can't happen—they're impossible no matter how much you want them." Daisy was pacing back and forth.

"Like coming to New York, living as a witch in the Bronx, and getting a part in *Cats*?" I said.

Daisy turned away from me. "What you're asking me is too much. I've done all I can do. I took in most of the stray cats in the neighborhood. I worked extra hours to pay for their veterinarian bills and food and litter and flea collars. That wasn't easy, Raven. Expecting me to take two strangers off the street to live in my house is not fair."

"Why?" asked Calvin.

"Because people aren't cats. They have problems and personalities and quirks. They're a whole lot of trouble."

"See, she said trouble. I told you so." The Raven gloated.

"These aren't strangers. These are people you know," I said.

"I *don't* know them. They *are* strangers. What's Windy's last name? Who is she? Where does she come from? Why is she hanging around with an old lady who is *not* her grandmother?" Daisy reeled off her questions at top speed, but The Raven managed to interrupt her.

"She is not *hanging around* with Miss Elvina, she's taking care of her—*good* care. And who says Windy's not Miss Elvina's granddaughter?" The Raven moved closer to Daisy.

"They could take care of your cats," said Calvin.

"And plants," I added.

"Miss Elvina does seem to know a great deal about plants,"

179

Daisy said as she removed a box of spaghetti from the shelf.

"Better cook up a couple of boxes," said Julio. "I think we'll stick around and talk some more."

"She's weakening, isn't she?" I whispered to Julio.

"Maybe," he whispered back.

"You'd be giving an old lady her life's wish . . . " said Suzie Q.

"Proving that Eldorado can be an attainable dream," Julio added.

"You can't possibly know what goes on in Miss Elvina's head. Her life's wish could be to live in a thatch hut in a rain forest. If I let them stay here, who would pay for their food—and the electric bill—and the gas bill?" said Daisy. "I couldn't have them living in my house and eating from garbage cans."

"You'd have to keep the electricity and gas on anyway, so the plants and the cats can have light and heat this winter," I said.

"Windy can use the hundred dollars for food, and I'll chip in my allowance every week," said Calvin.

"Me, too," I said.

"She won't take it from you," said Suzie Q.

"So we'll think of something else. The city will help out a kid and an old lady," said Anthony.

"If that's the case, why are they living in a deserted lot? Something is not right with those two." Daisy drained the spaghetti over the sink and put it into two large bowls. Anthony poured sauce over the pasta and brought it to the table.

"Dig in, I guess," Daisy said, eyeing Anthony's sauce.

"This is great!" said Suzie Q.

"You think everything is great," I said, putting a tiny amount of sauce on the tip of my tongue. "But this time you're right. Anthony, you're a genius."

"I know. I really want to become a chef like my Uncle

Cosimo. It's my *possible* dream." Anthony winked at me and attacked his food.

We ate in silence until we couldn't swallow another bite. The Raven was the first to speak. "I know what we can do."

"Find someplace else for them to live?" Daisy said hopefully.

"No, go over there and have Windy and Miss Elvina answer all your questions."

"What good will that do?" asked Daisy, burping softly into her napkin.

"If you hear the answers, I think you won't be afraid of letting them stay here when you're away," said The Raven.

"I never said I'd let them stay here," insisted Daisy.

"Yes you did," The Raven argued.

"No I didn't. All I said was that I had questions about their identity and circumstances." Daisy loosened the belt on her jeans a notch.

"Well, let's go get the answers and see what happens," said The Raven.

"When?"

"Now."

"You're kidding."

"I want to go, too," I said.

"You can't, Loretta. Mommy said don't leave the block."

"If they go, I go," I insisted.

"Me, too," said Suzie Q.

"We'll all go," said Anthony. "Right, Julio?"

"Right."

"What about me?" asked Rochelle.

"You can carry the reward money—" I began.

"Oh great. You trust me. I'm going to tell Miss Elvina that my personality is already changing and people are starting to really like me and—" Rochelle interrupted.

I cut her off. "—so if we get mugged, you get to be the muggee." I smiled my most innocent smile.

"Are you being serious, Loretta?" Rochelle's voice squeaked.

"Enough. You can make all the plans you want, but I am not going for another walk to the Wasteland at night," said Daisy. "And that's final!"

"It's amazing what can happen to an empty house in six or eight months," said The Raven. "Graffiti, broken windows, stolen rocking chairs. . . ."

"The Neighborhood Watch will keep an eye on my house while I'm on the road—and most neighborhood kids still think I'm a witch. Besides, they won't even realize I'm gone." Daisy's voice was a whole lot less sure than her words.

"You're right. By themselves they probably wouldn't figure out you're away. But what if word got out—if your traveling became neighborhood news, like the missing Princess?"

"You're threatening me, Raven." Daisy sounded shocked.

"I am not."

"You are, Raven. You're threatening her," I accused.

"It's all those nasty stories by Mr. Poe," said Suzie Q. "They've turned Raven mean."

"Edgar Allan Poe wrote a whole lot more than horror stories," said The Raven.

"Then why did you threaten Daisy? What's your excuse?" I asked.

"You're angry at her too, Loretta, admit it," said The Raven.

"Yeah, but I wouldn't trash her house—or tell anyone she isn't going to be home."

"What would you do?" he asked.

"Kidnap her. Force her to come with us. Maybe tie her up and carry her to the Wasteland so she could at least listen to Windy and Miss Elvina. I might do those things."

182

"And *that's* not a threat, too?" asked Daisy.

"No."

"Things were easier for me when you thought I was a witch," Daisy moaned. "Wait here and I'll get my witch's robe. If we're going to take a walk, we might as well be as safe as possible."

"Nice work, Loretta," said Julio.

"Nice work, Raven," I said.

"Those threats weren't real?" said Rochelle.

"What kind of creep do you think I am?" asked The Raven.

We washed the dishes while we waited for Daisy to return. She took a long time but when she appeared, she was fully made up and dressed as the witch of Burnridge. Every detail was in place—chin- and nose-warts, glowing contact lenses, hideous skull, and her smelly garlic necklace.

"You're looking particularly awful tonight," said Julio. "Would you care to take my arm and walk with me?"

"You just want to enhance your reputation with the neighborhood bullies." Daisy smiled at Julio, showing what looked like a mouthful of rotted teeth.

"That's gross," said Rochelle.

"Thank you," said Daisy, taking Julio's arm. "Now let me escort you out the back door. I know a way to get us off the block without being spotted."

"I can't figure her out," said Anthony. "One minute she's fighting us and the next she's helping us."

"Maybe she's crazy," said Suzie Q.

"Actors are said to have mercurial temperaments," said Julio. "They change their moods quickly and often."

"Julio, you are sometimes as annoying as Rochelle." Daisy pushed us out the door and locked it. We followed her down the dark alley.

TWENTY-ONE

LITTLE IS BETTER
THAN NOTHING

"I think someone is following us." As usual, Rochelle was trying to walk forward and look backward at the same time. She was tripping about every third step.

"You always think someone is following you. Why don't you look where you're going, Shelly. You're going to fall on your face and slow us down." The Raven whizzed ahead of us as we turned onto the Wasteland.

"Do you think they can tell I'm carrying the reward money?" Rochelle whispered.

"Who?" I asked.

"The muggers," said Rochelle.

"Sure," I said.

"Oh, no!" moaned Rochelle.

"Cut it out, Loretta." We were passing under a streetlight and I could see Suzie Q was trying hard not to smile. "Don't worry, Shell, I'll keep the bad guys away from you."

"Thank you." Rochelle handed Suzie Q a cookie.

"It's kind of like keeping a big, mean, pet dog, isn't it?" Anthony whispered into my ear.

"Shhh. If she hears you, she'll bite."

We crossed the rubble and knocked on the plywood door. Nobody answered.

"They're probably asleep," said Daisy. "They have no electricity down there. They probably go to bed early."

"We have to talk to them tonight," insisted The Raven. He banged on the wood and called to Windy and Miss Elvina.

We would have given up and gone home but The Raven refused to leave. He kept calling to Windy and Miss Elvina and smashing his fist on the barrier. "I know they're in there. They have to be there. They couldn't have gone away. We should go down and look. Maybe something's wrong with them."

"An understatement," said Daisy.

"The Raven is right," said Julio. "We should go into the basement and see what's wrong."

"Probably they just wandered off. They *are* homeless people, you know," said Rochelle.

"Is your mouth connected to your brain, Shelly? Homeless doesn't mean not wanting a home, it means not *having* a home. This was their home. Something bad has happened." I kicked the door as hard as I could.

"Shhhh," ordered The Raven.

A muffled voice came from behind the plywood.

"Is that you, Windy? We can't understand what you're saying." I was relieved to hear her speak.

"Go away." The words were a little clearer.

"You don't sound right," said Suzie Q. "We want to come in."

"Go away," Windy said again. She sounded as if her mouth was stuffed with something.

"Not stuffed," I said out loud. "Trouble."

"What are you talking about?" asked The Raven.

"We have to get in there. They need our help. Let's get rid of the wood." I grabbed a corner of the plywood and yanked. Suzie Q and Anthony joined me. Something was holding the barrier in place from the other side. "Let go of it, Windy," I begged. "We're your friends. We want to help. Is Miss Elvina hurt, too?"

At the mention of Miss Elvina, Windy let go of her side of the door, and we lurched backward.

"What do you mean by hurt, Loretta?" asked Suzie Q.

"See for yourself," I said, not really wanting to look at Windy but taking our one flashlight out of Daisy's hand and shining it on our new friend's face.

"Oh no," moaned Suzie Q.

"Someone's really messed up her face," said Anthony.

"It's awful," said Julio.

"I think I'm going to throw up," said Rochelle.

"Good," mumbled Windy.

"You sound like you're sucking on cotton," said Calvin. "Did you lose any teeth?" Windy shook her head.

"Windy, is Miss Elvina hurt?" I asked. Windy nodded.

"Then let us in to help her," I insisted. Windy shook her head and blocked the stairs with her body.

"It's fine, now, Windy dear. The bad people have gone away. You may stop guarding the door. Let our friends in." Miss Elvina's voice was strong and sensible.

"Are you hurt, ma'am?" The Raven shouted past Windy.

"Just a sprained ankle and a few scratches. I'm afraid dear Windy took the brunt of the attack while protecting me. Please come in and help us. Dear Windy appears to be in shock." Then in a voice that probably could have moved an army, Miss Elvina ordered, "Come down here, Windy, instantly."

Windy turned and limped down the stairs. I followed with the flashlight so I could light the steps for my friends. It turned out the flashlight wasn't needed. Lighted candles were everywhere—stuck to old pipes, wedged between the cinder blocks of the crumbling walls, propped on bricks, and lined up in a semicircle guarding the corner in which the two neat beds used to stand.

The place had been wrecked. Tables had become rubble. Shelves were in splinters. Food supplies were ground into the basement floor. Clothing had become rags. Miss Elvina sat in the middle of a pile of torn bedding, calmly filling a cardboard carton with what was left of her photographs and mementos. A purple bruise was starting to darken on her forehead. Her hands looked scratched and her cane was in two jagged pieces at her feet. She saw me staring at it.

"Got one miserable bully right on top of his rock-filled head." Miss Elvina smiled. "I unfortunately damaged my walking stick. Sit down, Windy." Miss Elvina patted the place next to her and Windy sat down. Then, winking at us, she said, "We are temporarily without chairs, but please try to make yourselves as comfortable as possible."

We found pieces of cardboard and some newspaper that hadn't been shredded and sat down on the floor outside the ring of candles.

"What happened here?" asked The Raven, moving as close to Windy and Miss Elvina as the barrier of fire would allow.

"When we arrived home from our afternoon visit, we encountered intruders—vandals—destroying our home," Miss Elvina began.

"It's my fault. I wasn't careful enough. They must have seen me leaving. . . . " Windy's swollen mouth made it hard for her to speak.

"It was probably me they saw, my dear. Besides, what's the point of blaming ourselves? We did nothing wrong." Miss Elvina put an arm around Windy, who curled up into a ball and put her head on Miss Elvina's lap.

"How many of them were there?" Suzie Q was furious.

"Fortunately, only three boys—about thirteen or fourteen years old, I would guess. A bad lot. Not from your block, I'm sure." Miss Elvina stroked Windy's hair.

"Why fortunately?" asked Daisy, who had been silent since the moment she saw Windy's face.

"Because Windy and I were able to rout them. If there had been four or five, we surely would have been overwhelmed and beaten more severely." Miss Elvina's voice shook.

"Windy fought them off?" Suzie Q looked at her crumpled buddy with awe.

"Like a gladiator. A knight in shining armor. An Amazon warrior," said Miss Elvina proudly.

"But they hit you anyway," Windy mumbled miserably. "They knocked you down."

"Think of what they would have done if you hadn't been such a tiger, child. You most certainly saved my life."

"Why didn't you shoot them?" asked The Raven.

"Shoot them?" Miss Elvina looked puzzled.

188

"With your pistol—the one you pointed at us."

"Water isn't very effective against muggers," said Miss Elvina.

"It's a water pistol?"

"Of course. Real guns are dangerous."

"Why would anyone do this?" Daisy looked around the room at the destruction.

"Many people believe that homeless people are worthless—that along the way we have failed as human beings and that somehow we deserve what we get," said Miss Elvina. "To many we become invisible. To some we become targets. Those who won't see us can't help protect us from those who wish to harm us. What happened here is a common event for a homeless person."

"But you weren't homeless," said Calvin. "This was your home. They ruined it. Can't we call the police?"

"You are a boy with a special soul, Calvin. Yes, this was our home because we had no other home. A cardboard box under a bridge is also a home to the person living in it. However, most people would see our home as an abandoned basement under an empty lot—a mistake of the wrecking ball. They would call us squatters and say we were trespassing. They would also look upon the cardboard home of the person under the bridge as garbage to be carted away." Miss Elvina sighed.

"Did you and Windy mess up those boys?" asked Suzie Q.

"I guess you could say that they left here hurting some," said Miss Elvina.

"Then you have to get out of here," said Suzie Q, "because tomorrow they'll be back with friends."

"I was packing up what remains of our things when you arrived. If you wouldn't mind, that pile over there is clothing that wasn't destroyed." Miss Elvina pointed to a very small stack of clothes. I handed it to her and she stuffed it into the carton at her feet.

"Well, that's about it," she announced. "Sit up, Windy. I think we should be on our way before dawn. We wouldn't want those people trailing us."

"Tailing us, not trailing," said Windy. "I have to think about where we should go."

"We'll begin at a hospital where we can get your wounds attended to."

"No!" said Windy. "They'll take you away from me."

"Why don't you come home with me," said Daisy. "You can both get a good night's sleep and make your decisions in the morning."

"I've never shared an abode with a witch, but thank you. We accept," said Miss Elvina. She and Windy stood. They moved very slowly, leaning on each other for support. I carried the carton which held their worldly possessions. It hardly weighed anything at all.

Anthony lit the stairway with the flashlight while we made our way outside. "Let the candles burn themselves out," ordered Miss Elvina, "and I would appreciate it if you would close the door behind us."

We moved the plywood over the entrance one final time and headed toward Burnridge. Without her cane and with her sprained ankle, Miss Elvina could hardly walk. Daisy made a suggestion.

"It's not very dignified," said Miss Elvina.

"But it will be fun," said The Raven. So Mrs. Jefferson Davis Hollingswood III—Miss Elvina to her friends—rode all the way to the alley on The Raven's lap.

"You're okay, after all," said The Raven as we left Daisy's house by the front door.

190

"They're only staying here one night," said Daisy, removing her putty witch-nose.

"I forgot to give them the reward," said Rochelle.

"Do it tomorrow," I said. "We'll meet here after breakfast."

"Don't come by until at least ten o'clock. I'm going to sleep late," said Daisy.

We walked down the path toward the street—and right into the arms of a crowd of parents who stepped out from behind the tree.

"We're sunk," whispered The Raven.

"Finished," moaned Julio.

"No we're not," I whispered. "They just think we were at Daisy's house. Act natural."

"Then why are they here?" asked Anthony.

"They don't look friendly," said Rochelle.

"Maybe they missed us?" said Suzie Q hopefully.

"Hi everyone!" I grinned and waved at our parents.

"Mashed potatoes," said my mother.

TWENTY-TWO

THE QUALITY OF MERCY

I felt the icy grip of my mother's fingers on my arm. "Is something wrong?" I asked innocently. My mother gave me her look of doom.

"*You!* Begin talking." Mr. Quinn steered The Raven under a streetlight, using the unbreakable back-of-the-neck death grip.

"Why me?"

"Because you're the oldest and should've known better, Sean."

"Come on, Dad."

"He likes to be called Raven, Dad." Suzie Q looked worried.

"Right now nobody cares what any of you like, Susan. Talk, Sean—or else."

"Third degree under a fluorescent streetlight—an interesting idea," Anthony whispered to me.

"No. 'Interesting' is going off the block at night—wandering around the neighborhood like hooligans—lying to your parents. That's interesting." Mrs. DeRosa, the woman who can hear a whisper at a thousand paces, had struck again.

"Hey Mom, how about some privacy?" Anthony complained.

"You'll get plenty of privacy when you're stuck in your room for the next couple of years. One of you had better start explaining."

"Fast," added my mother.

"Come home, Rochelle dear. These ruffians will be getting what they deserve." Mrs. Firestone wiped some soot off Rochelle's face with a handkerchief.

"I'm one of them. I'm a ruffian, too." Rochelle pushed her mother's hand away from her face.

"Bravo!" said a voice from Daisy's porch.

"Who's that?"

"Probably Daisy," I said, knowing full well it was not.

"Right, it must be Daisy. GO INSIDE, DAISY," The Raven shouted.

"Hogwash. There's no need to conceal my identity. You are all invited to join us for tea. We wish to have a brief tête-à-tête regarding your children." Miss Elvina held open the front door.

"Tea?"

"Tête-à-tête?"

"Who is that person?"

"Never saw her before in my life."

"What does she know about our kids?"

"What's a tête-à-tête?"

"A chat," Julio explained.

"Who asked you?"

We entered Daisy's parlor in little family groups, each kid in the more-than-firm grip of a very annoyed adult.

"I'm afraid there aren't enough seats for all of you." Miss Elvina waved her hand toward the sofa and chairs.

The parlor seemed small with all of us milling around. My parents squeezed onto the sofa next to Mr. and Mrs. DeRosa. Anthony, Calvin, and I sat down on the floor in front of them. Soon every sitable surface was taken.

"It's late," complained Mr. Firestone.

"For once I agree with you," said Mr. DeRosa. "Why are we here?"

"Because I'm afraid we've been the cause of all that has happened," said Miss Elvina. She was sitting on a high stool in front of the fireplace, balancing herself with a beautiful carved cane.

"Who's 'we'?" asked Mrs. DeRosa, looking round the room.

"Who's she?" asked Mr. Firestone.

"She's Mrs. Jefferson Davis Hollingswood III. I'm the other part of the 'we.' I'm Windy." Windy limped through the room carrying a tray loaded with cups and mugs. She put it on a low table before going to stand beside Miss Elvina.

Even though we had already seen her close up, Windy in the light was a much worse mess than Windy in the darkness of the Wasteland. Her arms and legs were covered with cuts. She had bruises everywhere which were beginning to turn blue. Her mouth was swollen and one eye was mostly closed.

"Oh Windy, you've really been wrecked," said Suzie Q.

"Was that child in an accident?" asked Mrs. Quinn.

"They beat her up," offered Calvin.

"Who's 'they'?" asked my father.

"Some kids from another block. They beat up Windy and

194

Miss Elvina and wrecked their house. Windy saved Miss Elvina from getting killed."

The adults stared at the battered pair. They had been so angry at us that they hadn't paid much attention to the lump on Miss Elvina's forehead or the scratches on her face and arms.

"Have the police been called?" asked Mrs. Firestone.

"No point," said Daisy, entering the room carrying a large metal coffee maker. She set it down next to the cups.

"And just who are you?" asked Mr. Firestone.

"Daisy Smythe-Von Root. This is my house. Anyone want coffee? Will one of you kids go get the cream and sugar."

"I'll go," we all volunteered, but The Raven yanked himself out of his father's grasp and beat everyone else out of the room.

"Is there a back door?" asked Mr. Quinn

"I'm not escaping, I'm helping," The Raven hollered from the kitchen.

"Why not call the police? Destruction of property, bodily harm, breaking and entering . . . " Mr. Firestone demanded.

"Our friends have not been living in a standard home," said Daisy. "I don't think the police will be very interested."

Mrs. Firestone got a sly look on her face. "Are *these* street people of some sort?" She pointed to Miss Elvina and Windy. "Are *these* the garbage thieves?"

"Mother of the mobard, I presume," said Miss Elvina sweetly.

"You could say they are under the street people," I offered. "They were living under the Wasteland."

"Nobody lives on the Wasteland—there's nothing there," someone insisted.

"Loretta said *under* the Wasteland, not on it." Anthony smiled his sweetest smile. No adult smiled back.

"In a basement," Suzie Q added.

"Windy fixed it up real nice," said Calvin.

"Is any of this true?" asked my mother.

"All of it," said Daisy. "Maybe the forest ranger would like to tell the story."

"Don't you think Miss Elvina should sit in a more comfortable chair?" I was stalling.

"I'm just fine, dear," said Miss Elvina.

"Talk, Loretta," my mother demanded.

"Mashed potatoes," said Calvin.

"I thought I was going to tell the story," The Raven complained.

"I thought *you* didn't want to," I said.

"Begin talking or else," Mrs. Quinn warned.

I began. The Raven helped. In fact, all of us—including Rochelle—pitched in. We began with the missing cats and told them everything. At the time it seemed that total confession up front would be better than being caught in a lie later on. When we were through, there was a long, scary silence.

Miss Elvina was the first to speak. "Although these children have broken a number of your rules, their motives were above reproach. I encourage you to be mildful."

"Mildful?" asked Mrs. Rodriguez.

"Merciful, Mama," said Julio. "she wants you to show us mercy."

There was another long silence. Even Calvin was too scared to squirm.

"In their defense." Daisy's voice made us jump in surprise. "They *did* take me along as a token adult. They were not off the block 'alone,' as it were."

All heads turned to face Daisy, who had stepped out of a dark corner so she could be seen. I was glad she had removed her witch robe and makeup before our parents met her. It made her seem a little more responsible—not to mention sane. Then I noticed—she had forgotten to take out the witch contact-lenses. She turned, and the light reflected off them into the room—like little spotlights from hell.

"I may not look it but I'm twenty-six." Daisy smiled. She had also forgotten to remove her witch teeth. It was a horrible smile.

"What is she?" asked Mrs. DeRosa.

"Does she have a disease?" asked Mrs. Firestone.

"What are you talking about?" asked Daisy. A couple of us kids pointed to our eyes and teeth. Daisy ran from the room. She returned almost immediately smiling a perfect smile. "Stage makeup. Sorry."

"What does that mean?" asked a confused parent.

Daisy explained how she got around the city at night. When she was through, there was an uncomfortable silence. My mother broke it. "Everything's been explained except who these folks really are."

"We told you," I insisted.

"No, you told us where you found them. We have to know more," said Mr. Quinn.

"Why?" asked The Raven.

"Because I say so."

"Don't argue with your father," said Miss Elvina. "I will tell our story."

And she did—at least part of it. Miss Elvina had lived in New York City for fifty years. She had traveled from North Carolina to the city as the young wife of Major Jefferson Davis Hollingswood III. For most of their marriage, they lived in an apartment on Riverside Drive in Manhattan, overlooking the Hudson River. She stayed there when he died. The rent was easy to pay and, as she put it, her memories filled the rooms.

One day, while crossing Broadway—a wide avenue with fast traffic, and a dangerous place for someone who can't walk fast— a purse snatcher knocked Miss Elvina down just as the light turned green. It was Windy who came to the rescue, practically carrying the old lady to the safety of the sidewalk. They'd been together ever since. Miss Elvina gave Windy a home, food, and clothing, and Windy ran errands, cleaned the apartment, and provided good company. They became family—something neither of them had.

Miss Elvina looked sharply around the room. "Just in case any of you gets any ideas, this child is *mine*. If questioned by authorities, I will swear that she is my granddaughter." Miss Elvina stopped talking and sat there looking tough.

"What does she mean by that?" asked Mrs. Firestone.

"She doesn't want anyone taking Windy from her," said my mother.

"Who would want to?" said Mr. Firestone, making a face.

"You talk too much, Firestone," Mrs. Rodriquez snarled at him.

"That's telling him, mamácita," said Julio.

"For now call me Mrs. Rodriguez."

"But I'm your son!" Julio complained.

"Maybe later. Right now we're waiting for more information."

"They were kicked out of their apartment," said Daisy.

"Why?" asked Mrs. Firestone. "Did Windy make some kind of disturbance?"

I thought Miss Elvina was going to hobble across the room and ruin her new cane by beaning Mrs. Firestone. Instead, Windy stepped in front of the old lady and began speaking.

"We were happy. We were good tenants. Then one day Miss Elvina—" Miss Elvina patted Windy on the arm and Windy corrected herself—"Grams got a phone call. There had been some kind of bad dealings at the investment company where Grams had put her savings. The small income which had paid her rent and her bills was gone forever.

"For a few months we lived on what Grams got from selling the furniture, her dishes, her silverware, and her few pieces of jewelry. Grams even sold most of her clothing to a secondhand store. Then there was nothing left to sell. We ate because Grams still got her social security checks—but they weren't very large. We missed one month's rent—then two. An eviction notice came in the mail. We tried talking to the landlord but he wasn't interested. One day we got back from a walk and the few things we had left were on the street—our clothing, our books, our pot and pan, our two plates and forks and spoons, our blankets and sheets, Gram's photo albums and box of keepsakes—all thrown like a bunch of garbage on our mattress at the curb. A couple of street people were taking whatever they could grab. I chased them away."

Windy continued in a flat voice. She and Miss Elvina went to the welfare office. They were told that there was a three- to five-year waiting list for public housing in the city. They were given some emergency cash and sent to a city shelter to live.

"The worst thing about the city shelter is there's no privacy. You live in a giant room with hundreds of other people. There aren't enough toilets or showers or clean sheets and blankets. If you leave your bed for more than a minute or two, people go through your possessions and steal what they want. There are lots of kids and many of them are sick. All night long you hear crying and coughing—sometimes screaming. Most everybody has lost hope. Grams stopped sleeping at night.

"We were just an old lady and a teenager. Others were ahead of us in line for help, for apartments, for moving to a private shelter. I could understand. It makes sense to take a mother with three little kids and put them somewhere safe. They told us we could take care of ourselves. And that's exactly what we did.

"I stuffed everything we had into shopping bags and we left. At first we slept on subway cars at night. We'd go to the end of the line and back—a couple of times. Then they began kicking homeless people off the trains. We tried the Port Authority bus terminal, but it was very dangerous—too many drug addicts and alcoholics willing to steal your shoes in the night. Besides, the police began locking the station after the last bus left. It was no fun wandering around the streets at three in the morning. I heard of a kind of town built by homeless people under the West Side Highway.

"Grams liked the idea because it was in our old neighborhood. We went there. People were kind. A couple of them helped me put together a little shack out of scrap wood and cardboard. We used our last money to buy some groceries. We shared them with our new neighbors. We felt safe. We began planning where we would rent a post office box so Grams could start getting her social security checks again. One week after we moved in, city workers arrived with bulldozers. They said that our houses were illegal. In two hours our little town was gone.

"That's when I decided to go as far away from people as possible. We needed someplace we could hide and be safe. I knew there were blocks of empty lots in the city. If we could find a basement, we'd be out of the heat of the summer and out of the cold in the winter. We'd be hidden. We'd be safe. Grams could sleep at night. You know the rest of the story." Windy took Miss Elvina's hand and held it tightly.

"Why didn't you call your parents and ask them for help? They must be very worried about you," said Mrs. DeRosa.

Windy closed her eyes and turned away from us. Miss Elvina cleared her throat and spoke. "Many children who are runaways are actually throwaways. It's not something we like to think about but there are people who have no use for the children they've borne. Windy is such a child. Fortunately, Windy and I have each other."

Windy grabbed Miss Elvina's hand and faced us. She stared fiercely into our eyes. "On the subways they called us the dirty people and tried not to touch us. I hated not being clean, but if you're homeless, you have no place to take a shower or wash your clothing or even go to the bathroom. I never got used to eating leftovers from garbage cans. I never got used to sleeping with a stick under my body so I could protect us if anyone tried to hurt us.

"Living on the streets is dangerous and scary and dirty and uncomfortable and humiliating and sickening—and it is a hundred times better for me than where I came from." Miss Elvina wrapped her arms around Windy.

"Now that you understand, I think we'll excuse ourselves. Daisy has been kind enough to offer us a safe haven for the night. Windy and I hope that in your wisdom, you will be just and gentle with these young people. All they wanted to do was help. Good night."

Supported by Daisy on one arm and Windy on the other, Miss Elvina headed for the staircase. There seemed to be nothing left for anyone to say. I realized that I had tears running down my face. There was sniffling and nose-blowing all around me. The subject of our punishment just didn't seem important anymore. Our parents took us home.

"See you in the morning," I said to Anthony as our two families dragged up the stairs.

"Hah!" said Mrs. DeRosa.

"Mom?" I said sweetly.

"Mashed potatoes," said my mother.

TWENTY-THREE

ALL'S WELL
THAT ENDS WELL

An entire month passed—slowly. Finally, for the first time since the night at Daisy's, we were sitting on the Firestone stoop. A much fatter Tipster-Princess Ponga, the Jewel of Siam, was stretched out in the sun munching on a pretzel she was holding between her front paws.

"This is great," said Anthony, "but I can't stay long. I have to catch up on neighborhood news."

"I don't think I could have taken one more day in my room with no television—and no snacks," said Suzie Q, who didn't look one ounce thinner. "My folks said they were proud of us for caring about people, but one thing had nothing to do with the other. Parents can be confusing."

"How about me? They wouldn't even let me draw on paper. I bet I've lost my touch." The Raven sipped his soda and stared at Daisy's house.

"They said if I elected to be a ruffian, I would get treated like one. They locked up my toys," Rochelle announced proudly. "But I didn't care—I had T.P. to hang out with. I wonder what her kittens are going to look like."

"TeePee?"

"T.P. for Tipster-Princess. She likes the name."

"It's not bad," said Julio. "Sounds sort of Bronx."

"Thank you," said Rochelle.

"I made good use of my time alone," said Julio. "I learned ninety new words, read eight books, and—"

Our groans shut him up. We had been hearing each other complaining on the way to and from school for a month. We were finally free. The punishment had ended. But, to put it all behind us, we had to go over it one more time—on a stoop— eating junk food. It was my turn. I had thought of a few more details to describe what a horrible time I had had during *my* month of punishment—being forced to stay in my room after school and on weekends—*with* Calvin—when the door of Daisy's house opened.

"This is it!" said The Raven, and took off down the block.

We were right behind him. When we got to the tree, Daisy and her two large suitcases were already on the sidewalk.

"Is that all you're taking?" I asked. "My mother said you'll be gone at least six months."

"Two are what we're allowed. No room on the bus for more. I packed tightly." Daisy looked at her watch.

"Are they really coming here to get you?" asked Calvin.

"Sure, but they're going to look like ordinary people, not cats. Actors don't wander around the streets wearing costumes and makeup." Daisy looked at our faces and added, "Usually."

A big blue and white bus turned onto Burnridge and stopped in front of us. The driver got out and opened the luggage compartment. He lifted one of Daisy's suitcases and groaned. "Why do actors take rocks with them on tour?"

"We're too poor to afford clothing?" Daisy quickly hugged each one of us. "Keep an eye on things for me, will you?"

"Sure. Good luck," said Rochelle.

"She means, break a leg!" said Julio.

"I do?"

"Actors are superstitious. You have to say the opposite of what you mean, or they worry," Julio explained.

"About what?" asked Rochelle.

"About having bad luck."

The bus pulled away in a cloud of black exhaust fumes.

"I wish we had gotten to know Daisy better," I said.

"Me, too. I like her," said Suzie Q.

"She's okay," said The Raven.

"Daisy is more than okay, she is splendid—"

We turned to see Miss Elvina standing on Daisy's porch in full witch-costume and makeup.

"—and so are all of you. Is your confinement over at last?" Miss Elvina smiled a witchy smile at us and cackled, "Hee, hee, hee."

"How come you're wearing Daisy's witch stuff?" asked Calvin.

"Tradition," said Miss Elvina. "Why don't you come into my parlor, dearies." She pounded her cane on the porch floor and screeched, "Windy, prepare the potions—we have guests!"

"She sounds more like a witch than Daisy did, and Daisy was pretty frightening," said Anthony.

"She's playing. She looks so happy," I said.

"Nice warts," said Suzie Q as she walked past Miss Elvina.

"Thank you, you plump and tasty child."

We walked through the house into the kitchen. I was amazed. The day we all got sentenced to a month of solitary confinement, Daisy decided it would be a good idea for Miss Elvina and Windy to stay and mind things while she toured the country. Naturally, none of us had been in the house since.

Someone had rearranged things so the brick room looked like real garden instead of the storage room for a discount plant store. The table, covered with a red-and-white checkered tablecloth, was surrounded by large plants and trees. The room smelled of baking. Sleek and shiny cats were asleep everywhere.

"What's cooking?" asked Suzie Q.

"Gingerbread men," said Windy.

"Who got baked?" I asked.

"Some stray kid who wandered too close to the back door," answered Windy without cracking a smile.

"I hope he tastes good," said Calvin.

"Heh, heh, heh," cackled the witch.

We sat around eating cookies and admiring the room.

"This is great," I said. "It's like having a picnic in the park."

"My mom said you're going to start school next week," said The Raven to Windy.

"Monday. I'm a little nervous. I haven't been in school for more than a year."

"We'll go together. You'll be fine," said The Raven.

Windy smiled at him. The Raven blushed.

"Love," whispered Anthony.

"What did you say?" demanded The Raven.

Anthony pretended his shoe was untied and ignored The Raven.

"Is your name really Windy?" asked Calvin.

"Yes."

"Who gave it to you?"

"I picked it myself."

"I like it." Calvin bit a gingerbread boy in half.

"Thank you."

"Would any of you like to help an old witch plant some daffodils?" asked Miss Elvina.

"Outside?" asked Suzie Q.

"Of course outside."

"But it's the beginning of November."

"You put them in the ground now and they grow in the spring," I explained. "I'll help."

"Are you going to wear the witch outfit in the street?" asked Calvin.

"Most certainly. It keeps the chill away."

We dug up the earth between the roots of the tree and along the path to the house. In the end, we must have planted more than a hundred flower bulbs, covering every foot of the small yard.

"They'll rest well this winter. In the spring, we will sit on the porch and admire the results of our hard work," said Miss Elvina.

It was beginning to get dark and we had to go. Suzie Q turned to Windy. "Tomorrow is Saturday. Will we see you at the construction site?"

"Sure."

"I wonder if she's been working there?" We were racing home.

"Every day," said Anthony.

"You find things out even when you're locked up."

"I have a knack."

The streetlights went on as we leaped to the top of our stoop. We turned to watch our friends go into their own buildings.

"Do you think they'll be here next spring?" asked Calvin.

"Who?"

"Windy and Miss Elvina. Will Daisy let them stay?"

"Forever," I said.

"How do you know?"

"I just know."

In the early spring, after the last of the gray city snow had melted, an amazing thing happened on Burnridge. We went into the street one Sunday morning to find a large crowd of silent children standing in front of the old farmhouse. Miss Elvina and Windy waved to us as we raced toward them. When we could finally see what was holding the attention of so many normally noisy people, our mouths fell open in wonder.

Every daffodil we had planted had bloomed overnight. Spread out over the little yard, wrapping itself around the base of the tree and shimmering in the sunlight, was a living carpet of gold.

"It's magic," whispered Calvin.

"It's Eldorado," said The Raven.

The entire population of Burnridge walked around smiling for the rest of the day.

MISS ELVINA'S VOCABULARY LIST

afterling—an inferior

fonkin—a little fool

fopdoodle—a simpleton

gundygut—a glutton

hoddypeak—a simpleton, a blockhead

hoddypoll—stupid blockhead

hoddy-noddy—stupid blockhead

huff-nose—a braggart

hufty-tufty—a braggart, a conceited boor

lennow—flabby, limp

mildful—merciful

mobard—clown, boor

whifling—an insignificant creature

whisterpoop—a blow to the ear

whistersnefet—a blow to the ear

whiteliver—a coward